EXTREMITY

EXTREMITY

NICHOLAS BINGE

TOR PUBLISHING GROUP
New York

This is a work of fiction. All of the characters, organizations, and events portrayed in this novel are either products of the author's imagination or are used fictitiously.

EXTREMITY

Copyright © 2025 by Nicholas Binge

All rights reserved.

A Tordotcom Book
Published by Tom Doherty Associates / Tor Publishing Group
120 Broadway
New York, NY 10271

www.torpublishinggroup.com

Tor® is a registered trademark of
Macmillan Publishing Group, LLC.

EU Representative: Macmillan Publishers Ireland Ltd, 1st Floor, The Liffey Trust Centre, 117–126 Sheriff Street Upper, Dublin 1, DO1 YC43

The Library of Congress Cataloging-in-Publication Data
is available upon request.

ISBN 978-1-250-37384-7 (hardcover)
ISBN 978-1-250-37385-4 (ebook)

The publisher of this book does not authorize the use or reproduction of any part of this book in any manner for the purpose of training artificial intelligence technologies or systems. The publisher of this book expressly reserves this book from the Text and Data Mining exception in accordance with Article 4(3) of the European Union Digital Single Market Directive 2019/790.

Our books may be purchased in bulk for specialty retail/wholesale, literacy, corporate/premium, educational, and subscription box use. Please contact MacmillanSpecialMarkets@macmillan.com.

First Edition: 2025

Printed in the United States of America

10 9 8 7 6 5 4 3 2 1

For Mum and Dad,
without whom I would never have had the confidence
to tell such ridiculous stories

EXTREMITY

1

Julia Torgrimsen: It didn't happen the way you think it did. That's the first thing I want on the record. I know it won't make a difference—I've been in this seat before—but I wanted to say it anyway.

And yes, I'm aware that "this isn't how it looks" is just about the oldest cliché in the book. I'm aware that you have a trail of bodies and the only thing that connects all of them is me. I'm aware of Occam's razor.

But when you know the whole world is going to declare you guilty, the only thing you can cling onto is your own innocence. If you let that go, you have nothing left.

I was lying in bed when it started, when they knocked on my door. I wasn't sleeping. I don't really do that anymore—not properly anyway. Sometimes I nap in front of the TV, or I sit down in the shower, with the water rushing over my head, and my eyes close for a bit. But a night's sleep, in a bed? That belongs to a different life.

I was watching letters burn. I still get them, even after all this time. *Fan mail.* How ridiculous is that? I don't even read them anymore, there's no point. Nobody left in my life has any business sending me letters. I put them all in this small metal pot and set them on fire.

It was 10:44 p.m. I remember because apart from

the little fire, the digital clock on my bedside table was the brightest thing in the room. The knock came again, louder and more insistent, and I lugged myself to my feet. I didn't know who was bothering me at this time of night, but they were certainly about to find out how I felt about it.

DC Mark Cochrane: I'm knocking at the door, and I'm thinking to myself—Julia Torgrimsen. I mean, fuck. *Julia Torgrimsen*, you know? The whole ride over I've been thinking about that criminology unit I did at college that basically dedicated a whole module to her. I wrote a paper on her solving the Ealing murders in '04.

DCI Grossman dragged me along because I was the only member of his team left in the station at that time, and he said something about how he was going to need someone to "level out the fury," but honestly I was barely listening. The moment he mentioned her name I had my keys in my hand and I was headed for the car. Jesus—I didn't even know she was still *alive*, you know?

I was staying late, getting paperwork done so I didn't drown in it tomorrow. I told Kate I didn't know when I'd be back, so she'd have to feed Lucifer, which she wasn't best pleased about. She hates that cat. We were meant to have dinner together, but she's used to me flaking by now. When we started going out and I was still doing my detective training, I told her, "Sometimes you're just not going to see me, you know? If this is going to work, you have to know that. Sometimes the job is going to take precedence."

It took a while for that to come true, before the *some-*

times became *always*, like it has been for the last couple of months. I'm not saying I actually sleep at New Scotland Yard, but it feels like I do. But I mean, hell, I'm working in *Grossman's* CID. That's all the big stuff—organised crime, murder, conspiracy. God only knows how I got in. They had an entry-level spot open up and I was coming out of training at the right time. They even made me do the Authorised Firearms training just to join.

Grossman's an intimidating guy, and not just physically. He's big, black, and like six foot two, and he's got that voice, you know? It screams authority at you. When he asks, you *do*. You don't argue.

So obviously when I heard him arguing at the station, my ears perked up. I know I'm not meant to eavesdrop, but when it's just you and your boss on the whole floor and he's shouting down the phone at someone, what's a man supposed to do?

"It's a terrible idea, Sarah," he was saying. "There's no way any good can come of this." And, "Yes, *yes*, I'm *aware* of that, but what do you expect me to do about it?"

It went on like that for a while, and without the other end of the call it was pretty meaningless, but I distinctly remember the last thing he said before he put the phone down.

"If it's an order, then it's an order, but I'm stating here on the record that I don't agree with it. That's it."

He puts the phone down, puts his hand on his head for a few seconds, then gets up. As he's leaving and putting on his jacket he calls to me.

"Mark—get your coat on. I'm gonna need some help."

"Sure thing, boss." I'm already on my feet. "What's up?"

"Murder. Maybe two. Get your car."

"Crime scene?" I ask, feeling my pockets for my keys.

"No." There's this resignation to his voice, like he's already given up. "No, first we need to go get Julia Torgrimsen."

DCI John Grossman: I want to start by saying I thought it was a bad idea, bringing Julia back in. I said it at the time and I'm saying it again. This wasn't my call.

I get why Sarah—sorry, Chief Superintendent Barrowcliff—thought it was necessary, but Christ, the moment she mentioned Julia's name I felt like a whole heap of shit that I'd been trying really hard to keep buried just got dug up and sprayed all over me.

What was it she said?

"No one knows these people like Julia does."

And that's true. She spent six years under the deepest cover I've ever seen in the force. She knows that whole world like the back of her hand. But that's not necessarily a good thing. We all know that. We all know how it turned out. Still, an order is an order. You've got to follow the rules, have faith in the system—because if you lose that, what do you have left?

But when I put the phone down the first thought that ran through my mind was the last thing Julia said to me. She said, "I never want to see you again."

How's that for a goodbye after twelve years working together?

That was four years ago, and now Sarah's telling me

to show up at her door like nothing's changed, like nothing's happened. *She's going to eat me alive,* I thought.

That's when I saw that kid Mark—that's DC Cochrane—at the desks. He'd just joined the squad, a month ago maybe, and he was wet behind the ears and a little gormless. There'd been a coffee stain on his shirt the whole day and I don't think he'd even noticed. Don't get me wrong—I think it's great getting young coppers in early. Train up the next generation and all that. But all I could think when I looked at him was: human shield. No way Julia tears him apart in the same way. Not a kid like that.

DC Mark Cochrane: When we're in the car, I can't help myself. I know I must be really annoying, but I have so many questions and I can't keep them all in.

"There's been a death?"

He nods. "You're not on this case though, Mark. Not yet. If you're needed, you'll get briefed later in the week. This is just a pickup."

Now I'm a little disappointed. But it sounded like some pretty important people were involved and I'm still quite junior. These things happen. At this point, I'm just happy to be along for the ride.

"You know Torgrimsen?" I ask him, keeping my eyes on the road. He doesn't reply at first, and I'm sure I hear a little sigh before he does.

"She was my partner," he says. "Long time back."

"*Seriously?* Wow. I mean, all due respect, sir, but that's really cool."

He laughs, and I'm not sure what I said, but he

doesn't follow it up with anything. I try to shut up for a bit, following the directions he's giving me, but I can't. The questions keep coming.

"Did you work with her on the Bankside serial killer?"

"Yes," he says, as if it's the most casual thing in the world. *Yes.* And I'm thinking, *Fuck, I knew my boss was important, but not like, a legend.*

"And the Peckham murders? That too?"

He coughs. "No, that was before my time with her."

"What about the—"

"Look," he interrupts. "Can you just drive?"

I mutter a little, "Of course, sorry," and nod my head in contrition, trying to focus on the road. But you know what happens like three minutes later? I start asking questions again, like an idiot. Honestly, I'm surprised he didn't fire me right then and there.

"Did you know her during the Yegorov case?"

At first he doesn't respond, and I'm worried that I've really pissed him off. We sit in what has to be the most awkward silence I've ever experienced for what feels like about five hours. Eventually, he says, "Yes. I was her contact while she was undercover."

"Holy shit." I don't mean to say it, but it comes out. I mean—Dmitri Yegorov—probably the biggest news story of the past couple of decades, from murder to paedophilia, to police corruption and conspiracy, right on through. The case that almost blew the Met apart. The case that sent police super-detective Julia Torgrimsen into retirement and obscurity. And the guy sitting next to me had been right in the middle of it.

The next question sits between us like a third passenger, bunched up against the gearstick. He knows it and I know it. It's the only possible follow-up question. Because if he was her contact, then he must know what really happened at the end. What caused her to leave the force. What ended her career.

I know the *rumours*. I mean, God, everyone in the force knows the rumours, even if no one ever talks about it. But to actually *know*—

Before I can say another word, he says, "It's another left and we're there."

There's that authoritative tone in his voice again. It's saying, *shut up if you know what's good for you.* So I do. I shut my mouth right closed. Practically stapled the damn thing shut.

DCI John Grossman: If I'm honest, I was really starting to regret bringing Mark along. So much so, that when we actually pulled over to Julia's flat I felt a sense of relief.

We stepped out of the car, and I said to him, "Look, she's not going to be happy we're here. I can tell you that now. But we need her, and if she sees it's me she'll just slam the door in my face, or worse. So I need you to lead, okay? Just tell her you've been sent to bring her in to answer some questions about a case. It's not an arrest, though, okay? And she's definitely not a suspect."

He was dutifully nodding, trying to take it all in, but I could tell he felt out of his depth. The metal gate to the apartment block was wedged open, so thankfully we didn't have to buzz up, and we headed inside.

We took the stairs because I didn't trust the lift. Rickety old thing looked like it could barely carry a fruit basket, let alone two police officers. I regretted that quickly. The stairwell was grim—cigarette butts scattered across the floor, walls stained with dirt and graffiti and God knows what else. A stale stench of smoke emanated through the whole building, which just about masked the sweet musk of spilt booze.

"So why is she being brought in if she's not a suspect?" he asked.

"To consult."

"Consult?" he replied. "But she's not police anymore. Why would she—"

Thankfully, we reached the second floor. I flung the door open and walked into the corridor, cutting his question off behind me. The long bars of fluorescent lighting in the hallway flickered and buzzed at us as we found our way to her door—8C. I remember hoping she still lived there, then I remember hoping she didn't.

"I'm going to stay just out of sight," I told Mark. "You knock and ask her to come with us."

He knocked and waited.

And I know what you're thinking. I do: I'm a chief inspector. I've been a cop for thirty years. What am I doing hiding round a corner like a criminal? But honestly, you don't know what she's like.

The door opened.

"Mrs. Torgrimsen?" Mark said, with that boyish smile.

"I'm not married." The flick of a lighter told me she'd lit a cigarette.

His face faltered a little, and I can almost hear him withering under her gaze. "Sorry, ma'am. I just . . . I mean to say, I've been sent to see if you'll come in to the station."

"Don't be ridiculous. Am I a suspect?"

"No," he said. "But you've been asked to—"

"If I'm not a suspect, then I'm not going anywhere. If I am a suspect, then I'm calling a lawyer and I'm not going anywhere. Either way, you need to leave."

"I . . ." he stuttered, and I felt for him then. I really did. But he was doing his job as well as he could.

"Julia," I said, stepping out from round the corner. I tried not to let the surprise enter my eyes. I mean, she looked like shit. Dark wrinkles, deep rings under her eyes, bony hands. I know she's only about five years older than me, but dear God she looked like she was about seventy.

Her expression didn't change in the slightest. She didn't move when she saw me, didn't react. Her cigarette hung out of her mouth, quietly smoking, and she stood as perfectly still as if she'd been transformed into stone.

"It's Bruno Donaldson," I said. "He's dead."

She didn't say anything at first. She just plucked the cigarette from her lips and dropped it on the floor, stamping it into the ground.

"Good," she said.

And she slammed the door in my face.

Julia Torgrimsen: I turned around and placed my back against the door, and a huge weariness came over me. It was like I'd been storing up all this heaviness—like a hundred thousand pounds of weight—in a box somewhere and someone had emptied it all on my shoulders.

Bruno Donaldson.

I walked over to the kitchen and took out a bottle of whisky—a Japanese one, a Nikka. I think I looked around for a glass for about two seconds before taking a swig straight from the bottle. I wasn't going to let myself get upset over someone who should have died years ago, but I sure as shit wasn't going to get any more sleep tonight either, so I might as well drink.

"Julia!" John was calling from the other side of the door. The cheek of him showing up here, using that fresh-faced boy to try and soften me up like I'm some kind of prom date to be wooed. "I'm not going anywhere until you come with me."

I sat on the side of my bed and shook my head, staring into that pile of burnt letters in the corner of my room. I wasn't going with him. I wasn't going anywhere near that murder. He could wade back into the muck himself. I'm still not clean from it.

"It's more than that, Julia," John said. His head must have been right up against the door. "There's another body. You'll recognise this one too."

I took another swig of the Nikka and I tried to concentrate on the burn as it ran down my throat. Of course he didn't tell me who the second body was. He was trying to get me to ask, to open up a conversation.

But I couldn't not ask. After all this time, I couldn't just *not ask*.

And then I saw the next hour play itself out like a film. We would argue, we would shout, we would fight like old times, and with every single word I'd be drawn in further and further. As soon as I asked him the question, the rest would be set in stone.

"Fuck!" I muttered, knocking back the end of the bottle and slamming it down on the table. It wavered, wobbling for a second before toppling onto the floor with a smash, glass scattering all the way across my flat.

Great.

I got up, my slippers crunching over the glass, and went to the mirror, giving myself a long hard look. I looked at my hands, balled into fists, and tried to ease them back to normality.

Remember who you are, I told myself. *Don't let yourself forget.*

DC Mark Cochrane: When I hear the smash come from inside the flat, I start forward, thinking that she might have hurt herself or something, but Grossman puts his hand on my shoulder and holds me back.

"Wait," he says, and I take a step back. But I'm thinking: *Oh my God. Bruno fucking Donaldson.* Surely, it can't be the same Bruno Donaldson as the one I'm thinking of—the billionaire tech giant, the founder of Altitude Computing and everything else that comes with it. Surely not. But then I remember Grossman's call and the urgency and secrecy, and I think about Dmitri Yegorov, and my brain goes: holy shit, Bruno Donaldson is *dead*?

The door opens. Julia is standing there, her face impassive. "Who's the second body?"

"It's more complicated than that," Grossman replies.

She rolls her eyes. "Of course it is."

Julia walks right past me—she's changed into jeans and a navy blouse, her grey hair tied back in a ponytail—and starts down the hall. "Well," she says, turning back. "Are we going to the crime scene or what?"

I see a flicker of a smile hit Grossman's lips. "We'll get a cab," he says. "Mark, you take the car back to the station and—"

"Oh no," Julia says, shaking her head. "You brought him along, he comes too. That's the deal. I don't look at this case without . . ." She blinks at me. "What's your name?"

"DC Mark Cochrane, ma'am."

And Grossman says, "He's not ready," which I think is pretty unfair, but I'm not going to say anything at this point.

Julia turns around and starts walking towards the stairs. "You should have thought of that when you brought him, John. Maybe you'll think twice about using people as pawns next time."

I did my best to hide my smile. Didn't work.

DCI John Grossman: Nobody said a word on the car journey over and I could tell Mark was just dying. He looked like he was about to explode, but fortunately he managed to hold it in.

I also knew Sarah was going to kill me when she found out I'd dragged along a DC, but unfortunately there wasn't much I could do. It was such a Julia thing to do—she didn't even want him there herself, she just wanted to punish me.

We pulled up outside the Shard. It must have been well after 11 p.m. at this point and the building was dark. There was a police cordon around the lifts in the lobby and I flashed the officer my badge before lifting it, allowing Mark and Julia through.

The lift took us up to the twenty-fifth floor.

"I've been up to the top of this building," Mark said, trying to break the silence. "They've got this viewing platform on the eighty-seventh floor, you can see all of London. Never really know what goes on below that."

"It's mostly office space," I told him. "There's the Shangri-La hotel above and then some residential apartments for the mega-rich, but that's about it. Nothing crazy."

"I thought the apartments were mostly unsold and empty?" he replied.

Julia snorted. I threw her a look, but she didn't care to elaborate.

DC Mark Cochrane: When the lift doors open, I don't expect to see so many people. I mean—of course I know there's going to be some coppers up here at the crime scene, keeping things safe and keeping evidence untampered, but there's more than that.

The floor is a wide-open office space with a group of bullpen-like desks in the centre. On the walls, there are about eight clocks with different time zones: Shanghai, New Delhi, Moscow, New York—all the big cities.

At the corner office, there's another cordon, but instead of police officers standing around it, there's men in suits.

I think Julia sees the surprise on my face, because she mutters, "Buckle up, kiddo," before stepping in front of me.

A man in a black suit with a sharp, angular face like it's been carved with a knife stands in her way.

"Julia," he says. His accent is American, with a Southern drawl. "So good to see you again."

"Pleasantries make you look creepy, Horner."

"I didn't know you were with the force again," he says, an undercurrent of threat in his voice.

"She's not," John says. "She's with me, as a consultant."

He raises his eyebrows and pulls a phone out of his pocket. He taps away at a note or a message or something, and doesn't even look at Grossman as he replies. "I didn't know we invited old friends to a crime scene, Mr. Grossman."

"Who is this?" I say, frowning.

The man turns, as if I've literally just entered his attention for the first time, and his gaze lands on me and, I mean *fuck*. You know those nature shows when you see a lion or a cheetah eyeing up a deer, looking for the weakest one to kill? He looks at me exactly like that, and he says, "I was about to ask the same question."

"Don't give him your name," Julia cuts in. "This is Norman Horner. He's a snake. Don't step on him. He bites."

"I'm a lawyer," the man says, with a click of annoyance.

"Yeah, yeah," she replies, pushing past him. She stops and looks back at me. "Let's just say if Satan himself showed up on earth and needed representation, you can bet he'd be first in line." She pauses for a moment, looking at me as if she's waiting for something. "Well? Are you coming?"

"Oh," I say, shuffling after her to the corner office while Horner stops and talks to Grossman.

The office is large and plush—there's a big sofa and bar in the corner, and a wide mahogany desk. The floor-to-ceiling windows look out onto the streets of London, but there's a big spiderweb crack in the middle, emanating out from a bullet hole.

On the floor, in front of the desk, is the body of Bruno Donaldson in a pool of blood. I recognise him from TV immediately. I saw him last, I think, on some news bit about electric and self-driving cars.

There's an officer in the corner I don't recognise and two people in suits standing around on phones—a young-looking Asian man and a blond lady in a black trouser suit.

"Time of death?" Julia asks.

"Between four and five this afternoon," the officer replies. I take the little notebook Kate got me when I passed the CID exams out and jot that down. It's small enough to slip into my inside jacket pocket and has a useful little pencil holder on the side. Back when I was in training, my old mentor used to say, "Write everything down, you never know what you might forget" and I've found it's really helped.

Julia doesn't look at the body—she goes to the big window and puts her back against it, looking through the door to the main bullpen, shifting her head this way and that. She takes two steps to the right, then back to the left.

"Wait," I say. "Surely there were other people here at that time."

"Oh yeah. Office full of people. Got about sixteen people who heard the gunshot. Got about three people who saw the blood explode out of his back."

"And no one saw the shooter?" I reply.

He shrugs. I lean forward and look at the body a little more closely. There is a single bullet wound in his chest right where his heart is. The shot went right fucking through him and into the window. And the thing is: the window isn't broken, not really. Windows in highrises like this are built super durable—they're basically bulletproof—and the crack on this one is on the inside. Whoever shot him was inside the building.

"Ballistics?" Julia asks. She walks ten paces to the door, stops, turns around, and walks back to the window again. The suits haven't looked up from their phones.

"Bullet is a nine millimetre, so looks like a pistol of some kind. But it's a little weird. We've sent it to the station for analysis."

I look up from my notebook, staring at him. "You're saying someone walked in here with a pistol and shot Bruno Donaldson in the heart and nobody even saw them? Look at where the door is, the angle of the shot." I point at the office desks outside. "They would need to have been standing right in the dead centre of the room."

Julia walks over to the sofa and looks underneath it. She stands up and spins around in a full circle with her arms out. She's still barely glanced at the body.

On the desk there's a computer and a phone in a plastic bag. I take a step towards it.

"What was he working on at the time of murder?" I ask. "Have we checked his incoming calls?"

"That's protected information," one of the men says, without looking up from his phone. "Anything on the computer or on his phone is confidential."

"What? This . . . this is a police matter."

The woman in the black trouser suit looks up. "What's your name?"

"Don't give her your name," Julia repeats. I stare at her, floundering. She walks over to me, grabs my arm, and pulls me out of the office and into the next room.

"What the fuck is going on?" I say, under my breath. "Who are all these people?"

"Lawyers. Personal assistants. Handlers. It doesn't matter. Don't give them your name if you want to keep your job. You're lucky enough we're in plainclothes and you don't have a badge number on you."

I shake my head, trying to process this new piece of information.

She sighs. "Do you have any idea how rich Bruno Donaldson was?"

"I . . . like fifty billion? Something absurd like that?"

"Sixty-two-point-eight billion. The rules have changed. Keep your mouth shut and try not to fuck it up."

She turns around to leave, and I grab her arm because I can't believe what I'm hearing. "Hey, wait. That's not . . . it doesn't matter how rich you are. The law is the law. They can't block a criminal investigation because they're billionaires."

She takes ahold of my wrist and pries my hand off her arm. "Welcome to the brave new world, DC Cochrane. Try not to get lost."

Julia Torgrimsen: I could feel Horner's eyes all over me from the moment I walked into the room, his beady little brain filing lawsuits and affidavits and planning calls to the superintendent and the Justice Secretary even as he was speaking to me.

I figured dragging a new young face along would work well to distract the suits so I could do what I needed to, but now I was having to deal with this naive DC who was as out of his depth as a toddler in the middle of the Pacific.

Yes, he was baggage, but that didn't mean I wanted his whole career to be ruined just for helping me out.

What bothered me was I still couldn't work out why I was there.

Sure—Bruno Donaldson was dead. It didn't bother me that much. I knew the man intimately from my years undercover and he was a horrific piece of shit. The invisible shooter was an interesting development, but not enough of a reason to drag out a pariah like me.

As soon as John managed to extricate himself from Horner's slimy mandibles, I confronted him outright.

"Okay, I'm here. Now who's the second body?"

John pulled out his phone and showed me a picture of another crime scene. This one was under a bridge somewhere, dark and dingy. The walls were spray-painted with shitty graffiti and rubbish lined the floor. On his back, in a pool of blood, was Bruno Donaldson.

"I don't get it," I said. "Someone moved the body here? Is that why there's no gunman?"

"No," John replied. "That photo was taken and sent to me by DI Lewis. He's in Vauxhall, where that body is right now."

"So it's what? A look-alike? A fake?"

"No," John said. "They've done fingerprint analysis. That's when they asked me to call you in. They're both Bruno, Julia. They're the same person. And they've both been murdered."

2

DC Mark Cochrane: For a little while, I watch Julia pace around the office like some kind of caged animal. I have no idea what she's doing. First steps of criminology are pretty basic: establish motive, means, and opportunity. As for opportunity, I'm as baffled as anyone. A shot from a gun in the middle of a full office that everybody heard, but nobody saw? It's like a riddle, or a magic trick.

Motive means going through records: looking at their relationships, their financials, but apparently we're not allowed to do any of that. At least for means we already have a lead—a 9mm pistol. I would have thought the next step would be to whittle down the specifics there, track down where one might have been sold or procured. Get in touch with legitimate and black market contacts.

But Julia's not asking any of those questions. She's got her back against one of the walls and she's shuffling along it, counting steps. I'm wondering if she's gone mad.

That's when Grossman appears behind me, thick hand gripping my shoulder. "What did Julia say to you?"

"What?"

He turns me round to look at him. "When she took you into the other room? What did she say?"

I blink back at him. "Erm. Not to tell anyone my name. To stay out of the way, basically."

He nods. "Good. Yes. Stay out of the way. In fact, maybe you should go back to the station and—"

"John." His head snaps round at the sound of Julia's voice. "I need to test out something on the ground floor. A theory, and I need a second pair of eyes."

"I'll see what I can—"

"Don't be stupid, John. I don't mean you." She cocks her head at me. "Get in the lift."

Julia Torgrimsen: Mark and I got to the ground floor before John had a chance to really second-guess what I was doing. In any other situation he'd have grilled me further, but Horner was making him understandably nervous. This was not a normal case and I could use that to my advantage.

Mark was staring at me. I don't think he knew he was doing it. He was standing next to me in the lift and I could feel his eyes on the side of my face. I turned and stared right back at him, my eyes locked onto his. He shuffled uncomfortably, muttering something like *"sorry,"* and looked away.

I felt for him a little, then. He didn't ask to be caught up in this, but he wasn't getting out of it easily now. I needed him.

When we stepped out of the lift and into the sprawling lobby, Mark started looking around the room as though we were playing a game of Cluedo and he was going to find an iron pipe under the reception desk. I watched him flounder for a short minute before he turned to me and said, "So, what is it? Why are we down here on the ground floor?"

I shrugged. "Because that's where your car is."

He blinked at me, confused. "What? I thought you were testing out a theory about the murder?"

"I don't need to. I already know how Bruno was killed. The question is who killed him—and for that, I have a lead. So, go get your car."

He was staring again. "Shouldn't we tell DCI Grossman?"

"I already cleared it with him. He told me to take you. Did you miss that? Where *were* you?"

"I was . . ." He frowned, shaking his head. "No, sure. Let's go. Where are we going?"

I walked past him and towards the doors, as he kept up pace behind me. "I'll tell you on the way."

DCI John Grossman: I didn't know why it took so long for it to hit, but when it did, I was pissed off. I mean—it had been four years since I last worked with her. You forget what people are like.

"Nazir," I shouted at the nearest officer. "Call down to ground—are Julia and that child there?" I didn't need to wait for the answer to come. "And find out how long ago they left!"

I reached for my phone to find Mark's number. I didn't think that he was intentionally running off with her. She'd probably told him some tale to convince him they needed to go. She's clever like that. I really didn't want to call the control room to have them put out an APB on his car if I didn't have to. It would be a colossal waste of resources. If I could call Mark directly and order him to turn the car right around, this could be fixed before it even got broken.

"They left about seven minutes ago, sir," Nazir said, appearing next to me. "Officer on the ground floor saw them leave."

"Fine," I said, "I'll just—"

I was still tapping my pockets—checking my front pocket, my back pocket, my jacket—when the realisation hit me. "Oh for Christ's sake. She's stolen my bloody phone."

DC Mark Cochrane: Now, I'm not a complete idiot. I know Julia hadn't cleared a damn thing with Grossman, but what was I supposed to do? There I am, in the midst of a complete madhouse of a murder scene, and *Julia Torgrimsen* is telling me she has a lead, and she wants me to come with her. What? I'm supposed to say *no*? Yeah, right.

She's staring intently at her phone—at a picture on it—but she's leant the seat back all the way so even if I glance left I can't see what's on it. Occasionally, she gives me directions.

"Left here," she says, barely looking up from the phone. "Then straight until the next roundabout."

"You said you knew how Bruno Donaldson was killed," I said. "Have you worked out how a gunman managed to make themselves invisible?"

She pursed her lips. "That's not the important question."

"Oh?"

"The shooter wasn't invisible. That's impossible. He was in the lift."

I frown, glancing at her. She's still staring at the phone, turning it upside down, using her fingers to zoom in. "The lift? How do you figure that?"

"Only way it could have happened. Lift opens. Shooter sets up round the corner, out of view. As the lift doors are just about to close, shooter lines up the shot and fires. If it's timed perfectly, by the time anyone looks, the door will be closed. Would take a lot of skill and training to get timing that good."

"That lift is almost thirty metres away," I reply. "Too far for a pistol, surely."

"Makes sense that it wasn't a pistol, then."

"What?" I frown. "But ballistics said that . . ."

"Ballistics are idiots. A nine millimetre from that distance means a rifle, which means it's Russian. That kind of calibre bullet is impossible to get outside of former Soviet countries, which tells us something."

"But . . ." I squeeze the wheel, shaking my head. "No. But there was no line of sight between the lift and the body, and there's the bullet in the glass. Unless the shooter can curve bullets round corners, I don't see how it could have happened."

"You're right."

I blink, a buzz of excitement running through me. "I am?"

"Completely. If Bruno can't have died where he did, he must have died somewhere else. Did you notice the floor underneath the sofa?"

"I . . ." I shake my head. "No."

"It had been cleaned more recently than the rest of the room. Far more recently. The wood was pristine in an almost perfect semicircle around the front. There was also slightly less blood around the body than there should have been for a man his size and an equivalent wound."

"How on earth do you know that?"

She brings the phone close to her face and zooms in with her fingers. "Experience."

"Wait," I say, wanting to look at her in the eyes, even though I'm driving. "You're saying he was shot on the sofa."

"Or next to it. There's a clean line of sight between the lift, the sofa, and the bullet in the window."

She puts the phone away in her pocket, and takes out another one. I remember wondering why on earth she needed two phones. "So," I say, the pieces falling into place. "Whoever was on the scene first took pains to move the body about three metres to the left, reset the scene as if it happened there, and clean up the original spot. But . . . why?"

"That," she says, sitting forward, "is the important question."

"So who's your lead?"

"Paul Merkaton."

"*What?*" And yes, you're absolutely right. *That* Paul Merkaton—the guy behind Merkaton Towers, Merkaton Hotels, Merkaton Resorts. "How many rich people do you know?"

She sighs. "Too many. He lives in Kensington."

"And why is he a lead?"

"Bruno's phone. Take a right at this roundabout and continue on."

I frown, turning the car. "I thought we couldn't touch Bruno's phone?"

"People like Bruno Donaldson don't just have one phone, not for the stuff they want to keep under the surface. Not for stuff they really need to hide. But I *knew* Bruno. I knew them all—that's why they brought me in. That Samsung with the silver case? That's the phone Paul gave Bruno to talk to him. It's a private line between them and no one else. If he had that phone on him, that's who he was talking to just before he was killed. You've got a gun in your boot, right?"

"I . . . wait, what?"

She looks up at me. "You're on Grossman's special squad, so you're an AFO. There'll be a firearm locked in the boot of your car if you need it. I hate going into unknown situations without a gun."

"You can't have a gun," I tell her. "You're not a police officer." She gives me a withering look and I feel like I'm shrinking back into my seat. "Ma'am," I add, stupidly.

"It's not for me, idiot."

I shake my head. "I can't get it out whenever. There are . . . rules. If there's no reason to suspect that—"

"The last time I followed a lead without a gun," she says, "I wished to God one of us had brought one. There was a fight. I was forced to use a knife, and the suspect pulled one too. Doesn't matter how good you think you are, you know who loses in a fight with two knives?"

I shake my head. She leans back and lifts up her top, showing a long white scar across her belly.

"Everyone."

Julia Torgrimsen: I let him take a good look at my hysterectomy scar before I put it away. It seemed to do the trick. That's the thing with most people—you don't actually need to lie to them. Put down the right pieces and they'll draw their own conclusions.

I knew we'd have a bit of time. John was never going to alert the station. He'd never tell you this, because he's such a goody-two-shoes, but I knew he'd try to find me all by himself so he doesn't have the whole station realise he's screwed up. He's so desperate to constantly appear supremely competent that he's utterly predictable.

Meanwhile I'm stuck with this kid and his barrel full of questions and I'm starting to think it would have been easier to get a taxi.

"You seemed pretty pleased that Bruno Donaldson was dead," he said.

"He was a nasty piece of work."

"Really?" he replied, in that same blind acceptance that everyone else gives. "He always seems so nice on like . . . TV and Instagram and stuff. All his money's in renewable tech and environmental stuff."

I rolled my eyes. If Mark was going to be a part of this investigation, no matter how small, he needed to know the truth.

"He liked to whip young girls. Boys, too, sometimes."

His neck twisted round hard and he gave me an incredulous look. I had to nod back to the road to remind him it was there.

"I could never work out if it was a sex thing or a power thing, but it was definitely a thing."

"What do you mean *young*?"

"Oh, age of consent, if you believe the paperwork. And that's how legal systems work. We believe the paperwork. The truth? Human-trafficking victims mainly, often as young as nine or ten, but paid off enough so that they and any families they had would lie and provide alibis. His lawyers tied the whole operation up in enough nondisclosures and red tape that it would appear, for all intents and purposes, legal."

"And you knew about this?" he demanded. "People in the police knew about this?"

I wanted to laugh at his naivety, but it came out bitter. His accusation sat heavy on my chest. "Do you have any idea of the mountain of evidence it takes to convict someone with that much wealth? This isn't a poor black kid with an ounce of weed you can lock up for looking at you wrong. Everything needs to be bulletproof. *Everything*. And even then . . . Do you remember the Panama Papers?"

He looked confused. "The tax-evasion thing?"

"Eleven-point-five million leaked documents demonstrating, irrefutably, a range of criminal activities from tax evasion, fraud, racketeering, money laundering, obstruction of justice, all the way to criminal conspiracy. Do you know how many people are in prison for that right now?"

"I—" he stumbled.

"Zero. A few fines here and there, but not enough to make a dent. And five years later, and no one locked up. Not a single person. The law doesn't work the way you think it does. If you're rich, you can get away with anything."

He shook his head. "That's not true, though. Dmitri Yegorov was arrested. He was taken in because of *you*, of the evidence you—"

"You know *nothing* about Yegorov," I snapped.

He was silent for a while after that, quietly staring out at the road in front of him.

We rolled up outside Paul Merkaton's place in Kensington at about 1 a.m.

The lights on either side of the gated drive flicked on as we approached, and a security guard with a torch appeared next to our car. Mark rolled down the window.

"How can I help you?" the guard asked, eyeing up the car.

"Police business," Mark replied. "We need to see Mr. Merkaton."

The guard shook his head. "It's the middle of the night. He's asleep. You'll have to make an appointment."

I leant forward. "Paul doesn't sleep before three a.m. Too much coke." The guard opened his mouth, as though he was about to contradict me, so I said, "Just tell him it's Julia Torgrimsen."

DCI John Grossman: I was pacing up and down the scene, trying to get a read on where Julia and Mark had gone. I'd asked Nazir to find someone at the station with his mobile number, but at that time of night most people were asleep. Julia had, of course, turned off the radio in his car. I doubt he even realised.

Meanwhile, I was still trying to work out what the hell was going on with Bruno Donaldson.

Ever since I got the call from Sarah I'd been on high alert. Then I saw the picture from Vauxhall—the second Donaldson body—and a big red alarm inside my head started going off. Something very dangerous was incoming, I knew it, and I needed to find out what was happening right now. The doctors currently had the body in autopsy just to check it over, but just as I was about to make some calls, and try to put out some fires, Julia disappeared.

I looked up from my phone and saw Norman Horner cutting across the room, making a beeline directly for me.

Christ, I thought, *I'm getting too old for this.*

"John," he said, looking like he was about to bite me. "Where is Julia?"

"She's back at the station," I said, and then, "I don't need to explain the movements of my staff to you."

He raised his eyebrows. "The station? Then why did I get off the phone with Paul Merkaton saying that Julia showed up in a police car outside his house?"

My stomach rose into my throat. I was trying as hard as I possibly could not to betray anything on my face, but every single internal alarm that I was aware of, and some that I wasn't, was screaming in my head.

Let me explain for a second. I was Julia's contact when she was undercover on the Yegorov case. Julia had spent six years with those people, working for Bruno, for Paul, for Dmitri and the rest of them. It had been a job she'd pushed to be on after she'd worked a case where some dead women washed up in the Thames. No one else could quite connect the dots, but she was convinced there was something nefarious going on amongst this cabal of uber-wealthy and she went in deep. Some of the stories she told me, well . . . I'm not going to repeat here, partly because they aren't relevant and partly because I don't want to deal with the legal ramifications of me saying them on record.

Dmitri Yegorov—that was her golden goose at the end of it all. He was running just about the largest human trafficking ring that any of us had ever heard of, providing boys and girls—mostly underage—to celebrities, to the rich, to anyone who felt like they were above the law.

Julia had to watch this happen for years, because even though she saw it, Yegorov was sneaky. Everything was run through disposable contacts, through handlers and little black books. She knew she needed incontrovertible evidence, and a lot of it, if she was ever going to take him down, and that meant she was in deep, with all of them. Paul, in particular.

I knew about everything—the illegal shit she had to do, the stuff that was redacted from all the reports. When I say Julia holds a grudge against Paul, that's like saying Tyson had a mild dislike for Holyfield's ear. The things he did to her. The things he *made her do*.

"John?" Horner repeated. "Still in there?"

"I'm sorry," I replied, backing towards the lift. I went

to take my phone out to fake a call, only to remember once again that Julia had bloody stolen it. "I need to . . . see to something in the lobby. Nazir! With me!"

Horner gave me that predatory smile, the one that tells me that he's got me bent over a barrel, but I don't have a second to worry about it.

"Where's your car?" I asked Nazir as the lift doors closed.

"Parked on the street out front, sir."

I put my hand out. "Give me your keys."

I was running the moment the lift doors opened.

Julia Torgrimsen: As Mark pulled down the drive towards Paul's mansion, I tried not to think about Paul as an actual person. He was a lead. A cog in the machine of this case that needed interrogating and moving on from. Whoever I remembered him as, whatever I saw him do, that wasn't the same Paul that I was speaking to that night. I couldn't allow it to be.

We rolled up towards the front, around a stupidly ostentatious fountain with a statue of a horse—I *hate* that horse—and in front of the main white steps.

Mark got out next to me, his gun nestled into his holster. He looked a little uncomfortable and I couldn't blame him. I was surprised he'd come this far. Part of me was a little impressed.

The front door creaked open and Paul stepped out in his dressing gown. He looked awful, which made me happy. His eyes were bloodshot and his face gaunt. He was holding a glass of something brown in one hand and leaning against the doorframe.

"Julia," he said, in a low croak. "It's been a while. Who's the kid?"

"I'm not here for fun, Paul," I replied. "Bruno's dead."

He nodded, then lifted his glass and looked at it. "I know. It's a sad day."

"You were on the phone to him just before he died. What were you talking about?"

He coughed. "Is this an interrogation, Julia? Come on, you know better than that. I thought they made you resign after Yegorov? I've already called Norman. He'll have the whole Met in court for this."

Mark put his hand up, as if he was about to say something stupid, so I stepped in front of him.

"There's no time for that, Paul. Something very weird is happening. Do you know about the other Bruno?"

Paul frowned. "What other Bruno?"

Mark turned towards me, and mouthed *what?*

"The second body," I replied. "There was a second body of Bruno found, like a clone or something. It's exactly the same."

Paul's face dropped, his expression shifting from confusion to fear. He took a step forward. "Are you *sure*?"

"I'm sure, Paul. I've seen the photos."

"And it's dead? You're sure it's dead?"

"Lying on the floor in a big pool of blood, both of them. What is going on here?"

Paul shook his head. He let out a long, deep breath and put his hand on his brow. "Bruno wouldn't have. He was so careful. He wouldn't . . ."

"Wouldn't *what*, Paul?"

"Shit. Shit, shit, shit." He shook his head. "Okay, Julia. Okay fine. I'll tell you, but you have to make sure—"

And that's when his head exploded.

DC Mark Cochrane: Just as I'm staring at the two of them, trying to process the crazy shit that Julia is saying about there being two identical bodies, there's a crack of a gunshot and Paul's head is splattered all over his front porch.

I stumble back in shock, splatters of red on my hands, but Julia is already in motion.

"Round the side of the house," she says urgently, pointing to the left. "Past the pool and right. That's the only way round to the back door. The other way will be blocked."

I stare at her. "What?"

"The shooter's in the house. I'm going in the front door. You go round back and head off the exit. Go!"

And she dashes past me, over Paul's body and into the building.

I scramble to my feet and start running, pulling the gun from my waist. My fingers are clammy, my hands shaking. For all that I've seen dead bodies before, I've never seen someone's head explode right in front of my face. It's not the sort of thing you brush off.

But the adrenaline has taken over and my training kicks in. I cut round the left of the house and leap over the gate. Lights come on. Cameras turn to look at me.

I pass by the pool, moving slower now—taking in my surroundings. I've got the gun out in front and I'm checking the doors and corners. I see the back exit Julia was talking about: a big set of windowed patio doors that are still closed.

Does that mean the shooter is still in the house? I think. *Or that they closed the door?*

Then I realise Julia is in there alone and doesn't have a weapon. Fuck. I cross over the patio and pull the doors open, stepping into the house.

It's dark—really dark. None of the lights in here come on automatically. I swear at myself, wishing I'd brought a torch from the car, but there's not much I can do now. Slowly, ever so slowly, I take a few steps into the house.

I hear the swing just before it hits my head.

I yank my hands up in time to stop the butt of a rifle. It hits my wrists and I feel a crack, yelping in pain. My gun falls to the floor, clattering on the tile.

Stumbling backwards, I refocus and see a woman. She's small—maybe a couple of inches over five foot—and wiry. I reach forward to grab her, but she swings a leg underneath like some kind of judo move and chucks me to the ground.

My back slams against the floor. My breath explodes right out of me.

She turns, ready to escape out the patio doors, when I reach out and grab her leg. Her clothes are all grimy and dusty, and she kind of stinks, but I still manage to pull her down with me. She almost *growls* when she hits the floor and proceeds to kick me right in the fucking nose, right *here*.

Yes—it's still broken.

While I'm screaming in pain, she literally pounces to her feet and swings the rifle round. She points it directly at my head and I fall silent. All I can think is, *This is it. This is fucking it. I'm going to die.*

"Mark!" Julia shouts, sprinting at full tilt from the other side of the room. The girl darts away, escaping back off into the house with the rifle.

Julia grabs my gun and follows.

I try to get up, but my brain's in shock. All I can think about is the muzzle of that rifle directly in front of my eyes.

Julia Torgrimsen: I knew Paul's house like the back of my hand, and by the way the shooter was moving through it, she did too.

I followed her left out of the back living room and into the library.

The house was dark, with just the reflections of the garden and pool lights coming through the windows. She was a silhouette, darting ahead in front of me, rifle in hand.

There was no doubt she had training: the accuracy of the shot, the way she decked Mark. She'd probably killed Bruno, as well.

As I entered the library, I lifted Mark's gun to try and get a shot at her leg while she negotiated the sofas, slow her down a bit, but she hurdled over them, barely breaking stride. I was breathing hard, my legs reminding me I was no longer cut out for a chase like this.

I needed to be smarter.

If Mark stayed and watched the back door, the front door was the only other obvious exit left in this house, but if she knew it like I thought she did, she might be heading for the small door out the maid's room at the side.

When we got to the games room, I fired at the ceiling.

She stopped on the other side of the room, glancing over her shoulder just long enough so she could see me dart right and into the pantry.

Let her think I'm headed for the maid's room exit, I thought. *Let her know I know this house too.*

She barely looked back for a second before she was off again. I burst through the tiny room and out into the garden. There were sirens in the distance—the security guards at the gate had called the police, not ready for a firefight for the rich bastard that paid them minimum wage. I put them out of my mind.

If she thought I was waiting for her at the maid's room, she'd head for the front door, and I could get there first by cutting round the house. A house like that— with its furniture and doors and adjoining rooms—it's faster to go round than it is to go through.

My whole body was sweating as my feet pounded gravel, climbing the outside stairs from the back garden and pushing through the side gate.

I collided directly into her as she barrelled out the front door.

We fell, tumbling over Paul's body and down the steps, and the first thing that hit me was the smell. It was a musty, dirty stink that I could have *sworn* I recognised, but she was already back on her feet before I could process it, running.

Pulling up to my knees, I lifted Mark's gun and pointed it right at her.

"Stop or I shoot!" I shouted.

She froze, metres away from me, and with the bright lights on in the drive I saw her clearly.

She was just a girl. Her clothes were a mess—a black hoodie with a big white star imprinted on it, and matted brown hair that looked like it was covered in dust. Her jeans were ripped and filthy.

I looked at her, I saw the fear in her eyes, and it all came back to me.

Everything I had been trying to bury under bottles of booze and packets upon packets of cigarettes. Everything I left the force to forget.

She was just another girl, maybe early twenties.

The same age Anna would have been.

I lowered my weapon and she disappeared off into the night, just as the sirens turned the corner.

DCI John Grossman: If you'd have asked me to picture my worst-case scenario, it wouldn't have even been this bad. As my car skidded past Merkaton's gate and down the drive, sirens blaring, I could already see something was terribly, terribly wrong.

Julia was standing on the front steps holding a gun, and beneath her was Paul's body, his head blown right off.

And I thought one thing, one overriding thought:

Christ, John. What have you done now?

As the car rolled to a halt, I leapt out of it, my pistol pointed directly at her.

"Put the gun down, Julia!" I shouted. "It's over."

Slowly, painfully slowly, she knelt down and put her gun on the floor next to the body. She stood up and put her hands behind her head.

I walked over to her, not taking my aim off her, and pulled out my handcuffs.

"You're under arrest for the murder of Paul Merkaton," I said, pulling her hands down.

"This isn't what it looks like," she said, her voice flat.

I sighed. "That's the problem with you, Julia. It never is."

3

DCI John Grossman: I was back at the station thinking about what lay in store for the rest of the evening. It was giving me a furious headache. Julia hadn't said a thing since I cuffed her except to ask for a lawyer. She knew her rights. When I found Mark bleeding from the nose round the back of the house, he opened his mouth to blabber something at me, but I'm guessing that the sheer fury in my face made him shut up.

I told him to get in his car and to meet me back at the station. This was bigger than both of us now. All I could do was follow procedure and have faith that the system would sort it all out.

That's when the coroner called me.

The ring of the phone on my desk almost made me jump, I was so on edge. I lifted the receiver to my ear.

"DCI Grossman."

"Hi, John, it's Rowena."

I sat back in my seat. "Any more news on the bodies?"

"I mean, nothing special on the one in the office that you don't already know. Gunshot through the heart. Dead on the spot."

There was a pause, like she didn't know if she should go on.

"And the *other* Bruno?"

"John—I don't know if . . . I just think maybe if you come down here you can take a look—"

I sighed. "It's the middle of the night, Rowena. I'm up to my neck in this thing. Just tell me."

Another pause, and this one long enough that it really started to make me worry.

"Ro—" I started.

"It's just meat," she cut in.

"What?"

"It's just . . . I don't know how else to say it. Under the skin, which looks exactly like Bruno down to a birthmark on his shoulder, it's just . . . *meat*. The whole body is pure muscle—no bones, no organs, no insides at all."

At first, I didn't say anything at all. What do you say to something like that?

"I know this sounds like a prank, John, but it really isn't. We've been looking at this thing for ages. It's like someone wanted to make a copy of a human but they had no idea what one was except for on the outside."

"Thanks, Rowena," was just about all I could manage. My voice came out small and strangled. This was beyond the scope of anything I'd ever dealt with before and I had absolutely no idea what to do.

I looked down at my desk for a second, at the lines on my hands, and the only thing I could think in that moment was how tired I was. Christ, I was so damn tired.

I got up and started pacing. I don't know why—the movement helped somehow. Just as I was starting to formulate some kind of way to respond to this new insanity, Mark appears at my door.

DC Mark Cochrane: Obviously, I have to clear Julia's name. I don't know what Grossman thought he stumbled onto right then, but I can't let her get arrested. If it wasn't for her, I'd probably be dead, you know? Now normally, I like to think I'd be able to take that girl, but there was something about the way she decked me. I've had the basic officer safety training—how to restrain someone, some baton training, and obviously the advanced weapons stuff that comes with being on Grossman's crew, but she's clearly far more trained than I am, or she's trained to be something very different. Something dangerous.

When we're back at New Scotland Yard, Julia is put in a holding cell while we wait for her lawyer to arrive. It's still about 3 a.m. and nobody is there except for Grossman, a couple of other officers from the Shard scene, and me.

Grossman is in his office, pacing back and forth. He's holding his head and it looks like he might be talking to himself. I've never seen him this stressed. When I was doing interrogation training at college, they tell you to look for the little tells that suggest someone's attitude to a situation has changed—the posture, the tension in the shoulders, the way they hold their arms and hands. It's not an indication of guilt, exactly, but it can point you down the right line of inquiry.

Ever since Grossman first mentioned Julia's name to me his shoulders have been so tight up against his neck it looks like he's worried his arms will fall off.

When we got in, he'd pointed at my desk and said, *"Sit."* Which I did, of course. But after taking ten minutes to scribble everything that happened down in my notebook and get my facts straight, then another ten of fiddling with my fingers and a picture of my cat, Lucifer, I just can't stay still anymore. I get up and go into his office.

I immediately realise I've made a mistake.

His head snaps up as I walk in the door and the look on his face is fierce. "What do you want?"

"Julia didn't kill Paul," I say carefully. "That goes on record."

His hand grips the side of his desk, like he has to steady himself. "Is that all you have to say?"

"Why is she being held? We wouldn't have even come close to finding the shooter without her. It was a girl—a teenage girl, I think. Whether we were there or not, Paul Merkaton would have been shot tonight."

He sighs, looks down at the floor, and then back at me. "Are you done?"

"Yes."

"Good." He straightens up. "Because let me tell you what happened tonight, from an outside perspective. From the perspective that Chief Superintendent Barrowcliff will see it, from the perspective that a jury will see it. While bringing on a decommissioned detective, a civilian, to merely inspect a crime scene, you—a constable under direct orders to simply observe—take that civilian away from the crime scene without informing your superiors. You then proceed, with literally no mandate or instructions to do so, to bully your way into the house of one of the wealthiest men in the country in the middle of the night, someone with a deep, complicated history with the civilian in question. Not only that, you get out your weapon beforehand. You give no reason for this. You leave no explanation. You tell nobody."

Sweat drips down the back of my neck. I open my mouth to try to explain, but he slams his hand on the table. The crack sends a jolt up my spine. "When the police *are* called—not by you, I might add—there is a dead body, a civilian using *your* weapon, and no other witnesses outside of a guard who saw the two of you enter and nobody else leave. Do you understand that?"

I step forward. "Yes, sir, but I—"

"At the very least, you should be suspended for your behaviour. In the coming days, there will be lawyers calling for your job and your arrest. I will defend you as best I can, because I know how manipulative Julia can be, and *I* believe you. But many won't." He lifts his hand and points at the door. "So go back to your seat and sit the hell back down while I try and sort this out. Don't touch anything. Don't say anything. Don't do anything. And if you're very, *very* lucky, you might go home tonight and not in the cell next to Julia. I do not have time or space for any more of your shit today. Is that clear?"

My face is red-hot with shame. I don't know what to think, what to say. All I want to do is defend myself to someone, to anyone. "But the—"

"Is. That. Clear?"

I'm looking at the floor. I can't bring myself to look at his face. "Yes, sir."

As I walk back to my desk, I see the lift open and out

steps Norman Horner—the lawyer—making a beeline for Grossman's desk. There's a grin as wide as a fucking canyon on his face.

DCI John Grossman: I was trying to keep myself calm and not tear Mark's head off. I was trying to process the case in front of me—the fact that I had three bodies, two of them impossibly identical, one of them some impossible Frankenstein's monster of living muscle. I was trying to work out what I was going to put down in the report I wrote once this godforsaken night was over when the lift opened and in walked the devil himself. I mean, seriously, it's like that guy had some kind of training in showing up at the absolute worst possible times. It's a superpower.

At first, I stood up, but by the time he reached my door, I was sitting down again behind my desk. I told myself at the time that it was a way of asserting authority, or reminding him whose office this was and whose station he was walking into. But honestly, I think having the desk between me and him felt like protection more than anything else.

He sat opposite me, his face now serious, but I could swear that he was holding himself back from licking his lips. Lifting his briefcase onto the table, he opened it up. Neither of us had said a word yet. We continued not to speak for what felt like a good minute as he slowly, one by one, took files out of his case and placed them on the table in front of him.

He reached over to one of them and opened it up, untying the string that held the paper closed carefully, and then he smiled at me.

"Mr. Grossman," he said, and I thought, *Oh great. He only calls me Mr. Grossman when he's about to bend me over the table and screw me.* "I'm going to need to have a sit-down talk with Ms. Torgrimsen."

I bristled. "There's no way I'm letting you in a room with her."

He raised his eyebrows. Ignoring my statement, he pulled a couple of pieces of paper out of his file and examined them as if I wasn't there. "I'll of course need to ascertain exactly what poor decision-making led to the death of my client tonight. Further to that, we will consider your resignation."

Now, I know what you're thinking. Who is this guy—a private lawyer—to come into my office and start threatening my job, or start demanding he question suspects? Except I could see some of the pieces of paper he was moving around, which I'm sure was deliberate. One of them was freshly signed by Tom Ruckland, the Justice Secretary. So maybe the real question you should be asking is *What kind of man has the influence to wake up the Justice Secretary at 3 a.m. to sign a document for him?*

I'd been down this road before with Yegorov. I knew exactly how real his threats were.

I didn't say anything. He picked up a pen and made a small note in his file.

"You can question her first thing tomorrow morning," I said, trying to feel like I was holding the line on at least something.

He didn't even look up at me. "That will give me an hour or two to call Superintendent Barrowcliff and discuss your continuing position as DCI. I doubt she'll appreciate me waking her up again."

My hands were in tight grips, my knuckles white. I almost said, *And are you going to tell her we found two identical murder victims tonight, or are you still pretending you don't know that?* But I didn't, because even though I'm not the one being arrested, whoever came up with the right to remain silent as a concept must have met some former reincarnation of Norman Horner.

His eyes flicked up and met mine. "I'd suggest you back down, John. You don't want to embarrass yourself again."

I sighed. My headache was killing me. "No," I said. "I suppose I don't. You can't talk to her until she has a lawyer present though. That's not my decision. That's the law."

"Ah," he said. He pulled a phone out of his inside jacket pocket and tapped a quick message on it. "Of course. My sources tell me her lawyer is pulling into the station now. Perhaps you could make me a coffee?"

I almost spat at him. "Make it yourself."

DC Mark Cochrane: The thing is: I don't go back to my desk. I know Grossman told me to, and there's a big part of my brain that's screaming, *you've got yourself in enough shit here, Mark. Leave it alone.*

But I can't stop thinking about the fact that Julia saved my life. I've been in my fair share of tense situations, mostly in training, but nothing prepares you for that moment where you're certain you're going to die.

And now she's locked up and it's my fault. She didn't do anything wrong. She was just hunting down the killer.

When I see Horner enter Grossman's office and watch them both sit down, I figure I've got a while before they're done. It looks like that kind of conversation.

I slip round to the stairwell and head down a floor to the holding cells. I grab the keys off the wall as I walk past and look into the interrogation room that Julia is in. She's on the other side of a glass panel, staring off into space. Her hands are cuffed in front of her and her eyes look tired. Her whole face looks tired, like she hasn't slept in a decade. She's not moving, not shuffling or shifting like people usually do in here—she's staring off into space, utterly still.

Letting myself in, I sit opposite her. She turns to look at me, but her expression barely changes.

"I . . . I wanted to thank you," I say. "For earlier."

She shrugs.

"I'm not here interrogating you or anything. Grossman doesn't know I'm here."

She smiles. "John knows more than you think he does."

I shiver a little bit at that, and can't help but look over my shoulder. There's no one there. "Listen—don't worry, okay? Without you, we never would have even *seen* the shooter. There's bound to be evidence at the scene that clears you. I mean, the ballistics alone will show that the gun you were holding didn't shoot him."

She raises her eyebrows, and looks at me like she's assessing me, taking all of me in—my face, my skin, the bones underneath. "You have a lot of faith in the system. Let me tell you something: until that shooter is found, you and I have nothing."

I wipe the sweat off my brow. "Okay, fine. So they'll find her. She's killed two people."

"Three."

I blink, and then the whole story of Bruno Donaldson's second body comes rushing back to me and I feel more confused than ever, like there's water rising up my ankles and I've forgotten how to swim.

"Y-yeah," I reply. "Sure. What I'm—I mean, what I'm trying to say is . . . she's not a ghost. She'll have left clues."

Julia leans in towards me. "She already did."

"What?"

"I know where she is, Mark."

"*What?*" I mimic her movements, leaning in closer to her until our faces are inches away. She smells of stale tobacco. "How?"

"By looking at what was in front of my face. It's something people don't do enough."

I only just realise that we're both whispering. "Well? Where?"

She gives a low chuckle. "I'm not going to tell you, Mark. You wouldn't know where to look. We need to go there together."

A frown spreads across my forehead. "You think they'll let you out soon?"

She leans back, crossing her arms. "Maybe. Maybe not. Probably not until they've caught her."

"Then how—"

That's when I hear some voices down the corridor, echoing through the open door, and I think, *Fuck*—I don't want Grossman to catch me in here. He'd flay me alive.

But as I push myself up and out of the chair, Julia's hands dart out and grab mine and my whole body shivers. "Consider the facts in front of your face, Mark. That's all that matters."

She lets go and I back quickly out of the room before I can process what she said. Grossman, Horner, and some woman are just round the corner bickering about something. I pull the door closed quietly and disappear down the hall.

Julia Torgrimsen: You know all the next steps. Alice—my lawyer—came and sat beside me, and then the one person I didn't want to see. Horner. He settled opposite me with his briefcase and started pulling out files.

"Ms. Torgrimsen," he said, every syllable dripping slime. "On behalf of my clients Bruno Donaldson and Paul Merkaton, I'm here to ask you about the events of this past evening."

Alice leant forward. "This isn't even close to being protocol, Norman. You know that. Let the police do their thing, and take it up with the—"

I put up my hand to stop her, and gave a brief shake of my head. I'd been on this side of the interrogation with Horner once before and I knew how it went. I knew the pieces he had put in place to be there. *Let him ask his questions,* I thought. *Let him try.*

DCI John Grossman: *This is why I don't have any hair left,* I remember thinking. I was in the bathroom splashing cold water on my face and neck, trying to cool myself down, to put some ice on my nerves.

It's meat, Rowena was saying in my head. *It's just meat.*

It's not about the threats from Horner. I can deal with that. God, if everyone running a murder squad stressed over every time someone asked him to resign, we'd have no one left. No—it was the fact that I had no idea what was going on and the thought of Julia and Horner being in the same room, even for ten minutes, was terrifying. The last time it happened was. . . . well, let's just say it was ugly.

I'm sure you've probably heard the rumours about the Yegorov case. The official story—the cover-up— was all over the news for weeks, months even. I'm going to do something pretty controversial here and tell you what happened straight. I know, I *know*. I probably shouldn't be putting anything like this on the record. But honestly? After everything that's happened in the past couple of days, I figure the only way any of us come out of this at this point is by being completely honest.

You see, after years working her way in and doing the dirty as Yegorov's personal secretary, Julia had accrued enough evidence to take him down for good.

And she did. You know all about it, of course. When the story broke, it's all anyone talked about for months. Julia brought it all in: all the little black books, all the recordings of meetings, all the witnesses that she had prepped, ready to testify.

We had him dead to rights. We had him good.

Then along came a spider—Horner and his team of hotshot lawyers step in and suddenly everything starts being questioned. Evidence is thrown out. Witnesses who were going to testify don't want to anymore. Recordings are questioned, deemed to be inadmissible. Piece by piece it all falls apart, and we all start to realise—he's going to get off.

I remember how angry I felt at the time. Looking back, I can't even begin to imagine how she must have felt. Six years undercover, enough morally questionable choices to plague her for the rest of her life, and it's all for nothing. He was going to get away with it, and there was nothing we could do. All thanks to that bastard lawyer.

Julia Torgrimsen: Horner started running through his version of the facts of the past evening, carefully presented to make me, Mark, and John out to be some kind of evil villains, but sound as objective as humanly possible. I knew his game: get me to interrupt, to argue with something and, in turn, incriminate myself. Credit to him, he was amazingly good at that—making the truth what he needed it to be.

"You decided to go to Mr. Merkaton's house based on no evidence whatsoever, taking a weapon from a police officer on the way, is this true?"

"No comment."

He looked down at his file and looked back up. "Upon arriving, you bullied his security guard to let you in, lying that you were there on official police business—correct?"

I bared my teeth at him. He'd done his homework.

He'd clearly spoken to the guard already, but not to Mark. Or if he had, he was carefully ignoring that testimony. "No comment."

"Is it true you also stole DCI Grossman's phone so he would not be able to get in touch with you?"

I raised my eyebrows. I hadn't expected him to know that. "No comment."

I knew exactly what he was doing, baiting me into defending myself, into slipping and saying something that he could take out of context. Because there's one thing that I knew as fact: nothing said to Horner ever benefits you. Nothing. That's a rule.

While he was speaking I pictured myself putting my hands around his exposed neck. It helped calm me down.

"So, to summarise," he said, looking up. "Since the start of your involvement in this case, we have already seen unauthorised weapons being fired, lies to cover up where you're going, thievery, and two dead bodies."

"Three dead bodies," I said, because sometimes rules are made to be broken. I leant back so I could see his whole body, every movement. He didn't shift an inch.

"Excuse me?"

"Julia, perhaps you should—" Alice began, but I ignored her. I wanted to see where this was going.

"There were three dead bodies. Two of them were Bruno Donaldson. There was an exact copy of him found dead in Vauxhall."

That's when I saw it. It was a split second, so fast that I would have missed it if I wasn't laser-focused on how he would react. There wasn't any confusion, any surprise, or any shock. It was *fear*.

He got it under control quickly, but it was unmistakable. He hadn't known about the second body, but he knew what it meant. And whatever it meant terrified him.

That's what I needed to know.

Without another word, he closed up his files, put them back in his briefcase, and walked out of the room.

I told Alice I didn't want to debrief right now, so she followed quickly behind him, leaving me alone in the room.

DC Mark Cochrane: I can't sit still. I can't think properly. I pick up my phone, flick randomly through things, and put it down again. I try to make myself a hot drink but my hands are shaking so much that the instant coffee spills everywhere. I want to look through my notebook, but all that will do is make me think about everything that went wrong.

Is this going to be it? Am I going to lose my job here, just because of a couple of little mistakes?

I can admit I didn't do things by the book. I can admit I was probably a little starstruck, but this is my whole career we're talking about.

Let me tell you something, until that girl is found, you and I have nothing.

"Fuck," I whisper, clenching and unclenching my fists. I have to do something. I can't just sit and wait. I'm too deep in shit already.

Consider the facts in front of your face, Julia's voice repeats in my head. *That's all that matters.*

And I get just the most ridiculous idea.

DCI John Grossman: We all had to come to terms with the Yegorov fiasco. No matter how hard we fought it, it was over. Yegorov was going to get away scot-free and we were going to go back to pulling bodies out of the Thames and locking away low-ranking criminals of no real consequence.

Sure, I wanted to strangle someone, but what could I do? That's the way the world works. That's the system. Either you live with it or you don't. You come to accept that when you've been on the force enough years. You come to realise that if you do your job, and have faith in the process, that eventually people will get what's coming to them. Most people, anyway.

When I told Julia he was going to get off, she didn't say a single word, didn't even blink. I assumed in time she'd just feel the same way as I did: angry, frustrated, but ultimately accepting. That was a mistake. I shouldn't have made any assumptions about Julia after what she went through, after what she saw.

By the time I realised what was happening it was too late. I was in the station at the time—quite a few of us were. She didn't seem to care. I remember clocking her grabbing the keys to the holding cells. Yegorov had been brought in for one final deposition—a kind of conclusive summary of the case before it was all tied up. It wasn't even going to go to court.

For a while, I remember thinking, *That's odd. Why's she going to talk to Yegorov?*

I made myself a coffee. I sat at my desk and thought about some other things.

When it hit me, I ran as fast as I could, leaping down the steps three at a time. I burst into the cell too late.

Dmitri Yegorov was sitting at the table in the centre of the room, dead. His face was blue and purple and his tie was tight around his neck.

Julia was right behind him, holding the noose.

Everyone on duty at the station that night was on Julia's side, even if it made them morally uncomfortable. Everyone knew her, respected her, and Yegorov was a monster. No one was going to be sad about him passing, but we needed a plan.

So we agreed to cover it up. We all knew how investigations worked. We all knew what to hide, how to make it look like Julia hadn't been there that night, provide her an alibi. How to make it look like he committed suicide. That was the official story—suicide, wracked with guilt at what he had done. *Guilt*. Oh, the irony.

And yes, I'm aware I'm admitting to my involvement in the conspiracy here, but after the last day or two, it seems pretty small in comparison. The context is . . . well, it's necessary. If you want to understand how this all went down, you have to understand Julia.

I tried to talk to her about it after the fact, because while I could empathise with wanting to kill that cockroach, I could never shake the idea that there was something deeper going on between them I didn't understand. Something I had missed.

It didn't matter. Julia resigned and never came back.

Not until the day I decided to bring her back, and now I had three more bodies on my hands.

And the *one* thing that was keeping me from exploding in that moment was that I knew where Julia was, that she was safe, and that she couldn't do anything else to screw this up any more than it already was.

Julia Torgrimsen: When the door opened again, I smiled. I had expected Mark to take a bit longer than this, if I'm being honest. He was growing in my estimation, I'll give him that.

He bustled into the room, his movements all jerky and anxious, looking over his shoulder. Taking a key out of his pocket, he uncuffed me.

"What the fuck am I doing?" he muttered, more to himself than me. "I don't know what the fuck I'm doing."

"You know exactly what you're doing, Mark," I said softly, as I got up and stood next to him. I looked him right in the eyes. "Tell me."

He stopped, staring back at me, and took a deep breath. "I'm breaking you out."

"Damn right you are," I replied. "Now let's go find ourselves a killer."

4

DC Mark Cochrane: So there I am—driving through the London streets in what is probably now a stolen police car, expecting an APB to be put out on us at any moment. It's not until Julia tells me that we need to ditch the car and take another one that I realise quite how far out of my depth I am.

"It can't be your own," Julia says. "It'll be on file. They'll be looking for that immediately. What other cars do you have access to?"

"What other . . ." I stumble over my words. "What kind of question is that? What kind of person has access to multiple cars?"

She closes her eyes for a moment, as if to say, *God help me this guy is slow*, then asks: "You have a wife, or a girlfriend?"

"Sure, but I—"

"Does she have a car? Can you find a set of keys?"

"Well, yes. But I'm . . . I'm not on the insurance."

She looks at me with a hard stare. "You've broken a suspect out of a police station."

I shake my head. "Christ."

And yet, despite it all, I feel this intense thrill. It's like I'm in a James Bond film, or a spy show. We roll up to the street opposite my house and I cross the road and sneak inside, touching the door closed, tiptoeing, not waking Kate up. I get the keys in a flash and before I know it, we're out—cars switched.

Julia Torgrimsen: He had about as much stealth as a rhinoceros. He pretty much slammed the front door. He crashed about his house for what felt like an age. I was certain he was going to wake his girlfriend up and we'd have to deal with that whole situation.

Somehow, miraculously, she slept through it.

I wondered if she might actually be dead.

DC Mark Cochrane: It's ridiculous that the only thing in my mind as I'm driving is that Kate's going to be really pissed off that I've adjusted the driver's seat. She makes such a deal about getting it in exactly the right position. I reckon by worrying about the small stuff I can push the really big stuff right to the back of my mind. You know—losing my job, getting arrested, trying to find a trained killer who almost shot me earlier this evening. All that stuff.

"We're heading north," she says. "Up near Marylebone."

"How do you know where to go?"

Julia shrugs. "Luck. I recognised her hoodie."

"You . . . recognised her hoodie? And that told you where she was?"

She nods. "Black hoodie with the star on it. I've seen it before. There's a secondhand shop near Marylebone that stencils that star onto every single piece of clothing they sell. It's a brand thing. Plus, I pulled this off it when we tussled."

She pulls a label out of her pocket that says WHITE STAR CLOTHES, £13.99.

I laugh. "Seriously? You saw her for like two seconds, in the *dark*, at the Merkaton place. How on earth did you see that on her?"

"It wasn't that dark," she replies, and doesn't add anything else. I'm trying not to gape at her like she's some kind of genius. I reckon it's like driving, you know? I heard about this test when I was in training—one of those videos they make you watch that feels like it's ten years long. Anyway, they've done tests on first-time drivers, give them a snapshot of a road for a second and ask them how many details they can remember and it's usually like three to five. But do it with someone who's been driving ten years and it's more like twenty. It's an experience thing—your subconscious brain learns to pick up the stuff your conscious brain doesn't realise is important right away. Julia's been doing this long enough her brain just takes in the information it needs. There's no training that can replace that kind of experience.

"And why do you think she'll go back there? Anyone can pop in to a charity shop."

"Most people don't go shopping throughout London to find secondhand clothes in charity shops."

I raise my eyebrows. "That's a big assumption."

"Think about it: she's killing some of the wealthiest, most well-connected people in the world. She can't be living in broad daylight. When she needs something, like clothes, she'll go to the nearest possible shop—the one that requires the least amount of time in public. And then there was the dust."

"The dust?"

"Her clothes and hair were covered in it, like she's been sleeping in an old abandoned building or construction site with no access to a shower. And the smell. Did you smell her?"

"I . . ." I frown, a little confused. "Not really my focus. I guess she was kind of . . . vinegary?"

"Acetate," Julia says. "Very distinctive, used in glues and nail polish removers. Have it sitting around in tubs and pots and it'll permeate anything." She taps something into her phone. "Quick search and it turns out there's an old abandoned warehouse that used to store acetate for local distributors before they went under in the financial crash, and it's just one block back from that clothes shop. I'd put money on them leaving the rest of their stock behind when they left, and I'd also bet that's where she's holed up."

"All this from her clothes?"

She clicks her tongue in annoyance. "No, Mark. All this from observation, logic, and deduction, through making creative links and seeing patterns. Don't downplay what we do. That's the first lesson. Despite what they might have told you at college, detection isn't grunt work. It's art."

Julia Torgrimsen: He was asking me questions and I can't remember what I replied. All I know is my mind was focused on the girl.

There was no question that someone would have had motive to kill Bruno and Paul. God—*I* had motive to kill them. What I was stuck on was how methodical, how well trained she appeared to be. This was no mere trafficking victim out for revenge. I recognised the rifle from the house—a modified Russian AK-9 with a suppressor on it, intended for covert work. Even without the dead clone, I could tell there was something much larger going on here than a crime of passion or a revenge spree.

And yet beneath all of that, I couldn't get her face out of my head. She'd taken out two, sorry, *three* targets with military precision and she had looked . . . I don't know. Trapped. All I could think at the time was *I've seen that look before. That exact same look.*

It was the look Anna had on her face just before I let her die. Before the incident with Yegorov in that interrogation room, and everything that followed.

That worried me, because there's something about hunting a suspect that needs a touch of killer instinct. It dips down into that primordial caveman hunter part of the brain. Lion hunts gazelle. Cat kills mouse.

If I was going into this thinking about her as a victim, then I wouldn't be able to see her as a predator. And given her track record so far, that was about the most dangerous mistake I could make.

DCI John Grossman: Okay, so this is not the way Julia would tell it, I'm sure, but when Horner stepped out of the room with Julia's lawyer, I was expecting to see some kind of look of triumph on his face. To be honest, I was expecting him to come straight back into my office and lord whatever had happened over me. I was readying myself for it.

But he didn't.

Instead, I saw something that if you'd told me a month ago, I would have laughed in your face. Horner was *shaken*.

I intercepted him as he made his way to the lift.

"Good talk?" I asked. He blinked, looking at me as if he'd forgotten who I was.

"Oh," he said, stumbling. Horner never stumbled. I didn't think he could stumble. "Yes. I just need to clarify some details on Bruno's case."

"Bruno's case?" I asked. "I thought you were here because of Paul?"

He frowned, then shook his head. Without another word to me, he hurried himself into the lift.

I've worked murder cases for twelve years. I've come into contact with Horner on and off for a good decade of that. The man is a world-class poker player. He knows how to hide his tells better than anyone I've ever met.

But something had happened in there, something so big that he wasn't even thinking about trying to hide it. It was taking all of his brain and then some. I've seen it before, in jail cells and courtrooms when they don't think you're looking—the shuffling of his steps, the clench of his hands, the stricken blankness on his face. He was *guilty*.

But of what?

I darted to the stairs, knowing that if I took them three at a time I could make the car park before that old trundling lift did. Julia was locked in her room, and Mark—for all he'd been an idiot tonight—was just about recalcitrant and competent enough to keep to himself.

When I got to the car park, I shuffled out the door and hid behind a pillar.

Something about tonight was wrong—more wrong than I'd thought. The call from the coroner, and now seeing Horner like that, I felt like this whole investigation was taking place on a lake with very thin ice, and there was a whole deep black body of *wrong* underneath us that we couldn't see because we weren't looking at it.

Horner got into his car and turned on the engine. I waited for him to get to the end of the car park and put his ticket into the machine before I darted to mine.

Wherever he was going, I was going to be right behind him.

And you want to know the truth? It felt *good*. Despite the worry and the stress and the nervousness, there was something liberating about tailing a suspect. Ever since I made DCI, the job has been increasingly the shit stuff: paperwork, spreadsheets, meeting with superiors and discussions of quotas and hiring and stats. It's all the stuff I hated when I was a DC like Mark. I loved being on the chase, working a lead, following a suspect. I was good at it.

I gripped the steering wheel in my hands, feeling the light touch of the pedal underneath me. I took a long breath.

Tailing someone with one car is much harder than it looks in films. By yourself, it's almost impossible to stay on the tail of someone with a tiny modicum of situational awareness without either being seen or losing them. A police tail would normally have at least four cars, all working in tandem and on the radio, dipping in and out. I didn't have that luxury. It was God knows what hour in the morning and none of this had been planned or approved, so I had to wing it.

The only way you keep on a car by yourself is by a frankly astounding mixture of luck, improvisation, and ingenuity. You have to watch the way the car moves, the slight touches in the steering on the road, the tiny little tells that indicate whether it'll come off the motorway soon or stay on until the next junction. You need to know every street and back road like the back of your hand. You've got to work out where the car is going before it gets there, and take separate routes. Cut around corners. Make wild guesses.

It's not something that can be taught. It's not something that should be taught, given how prone it is to failure. But, at the risk of sounding arrogant, on a good night with the wind in my favour, it's something I can do.

After three correct guesses, I made my first miss. I was certain he was going to turn left at the next roundabout, up towards Marble Arch, so I took an earlier junction to meet him halfway. His car was nowhere to be seen.

Goddamnit, I thought, and swerved round, slamming on the lights and siren. It didn't matter now—he hadn't taken a left and he'd be nowhere near me. There was no way he would have taken the right: the recent roadworks make that either a dead end or a circle back towards the station. So he had gone straight on, towards Islington.

I beat down the roads, zooming at eighty through residential streets. If the traffic and lights were shit and I could get there quick, I could still catch up with him.

Just before I turned into Islington, I turned off the siren.

The streets were quiet. If he was here, I would find him.

Julia Torgrimsen: Fortunately there were two torches in the car, because when we got to the abandoned warehouse, it was pitch-black. Windows had been covered by cardboard and the strip lights had no power. The place stunk with that sharp tang of acetate, and a quick flick of the torch showed poorly kept tubs of the stuff all over the place. The only sounds were our footsteps and the low hum of the streets outside. It was like walking into a mausoleum.

I've been in abandoned buildings before. They have a feel to them, especially blacked out like this—they press in on you, pushing you down, making you feel like you're trapped. But Mark clearly hadn't, because his whole body was shaking. I could hear his teeth chattering.

"It's a bit cold," he said.

I reached over and grabbed his shaking torch. "Keep your light steady. This is a hunt, not a disco."

Ten minutes in, we'd seen nothing. No hints. No clues. We'd worked our way around the ground floor and slowly up the stairs. There were four floors and my guess was that she'd be on the second or above to get a good vantage point of the street below. If we found nothing, we'd circle back and loop through again.

We were on the first floor, making our way into a large empty room just off the stairwell. I touched Mark's shoulder and he almost jumped out of his skin.

"Easy, soldier," I said. "We need to turn round. We should—"

There was a slight shuffle off to our left. I spun my torch round, but caught nothing.

"What is it?" Mark whispered. My hand flew to his mouth.

Shut up, I thought. She was following us. I was certain of it, and we'd been signalling our location with our huge fucking beacons of light the entire way, showing her exactly where to hide to stay out of sight.

I turned off my torch, then reached over and turned off his, plunging us into darkness. Even the playing field a little. Mark's whole body tensed up.

The two of us stood in the black for ten seconds, then thirty, listening. Mark was breathing so fucking loud I wanted to strangle him. I tightened my grip on his wrist to make do.

I closed my eyes, not letting my brain rely on sight at all. Just sounds. Just movement.

Then I heard it. Another shuffle, at my seven o'clock.

I pointed the torch directly at it and turned it on.

DC Mark Cochrane: I'm shivering in the dark, with no fucking clue what we're doing. The place reeks of sickly sweet vinegar and paint stripper. Julia's hand is so fucking tight on my wrist I swear she's about to wrench it off. It's all I can do not to yelp in pain—for an older lady, she's got some muscle.

I've not said anything, but I'm absolutely shitting myself in here. I hate the dark, always have, and the claustrophobia of these blacked-out windows is really not helping.

Then she flicks her torch on and there—in the circle of suddenly bright light—is the girl, caught like a deer in headlights.

She bursts into a run, heading right. Julia's hand immediately lets go and she's moving. I follow, charging after her, when I see Julia's torch go left.

I freeze, swinging my light round. The dash right was a feint, I realise—she's trying to get out of our light.

But Julia's on her, moving fast towards the stairwell, and I'm chasing behind. I put my torch on the widest setting possible, pulling a little behind them so that I can illuminate as much of the space as I can. She's already headed up the stairs, footsteps slapping against the floor, and I'm having to jump over empty cans of paint or whatever that are littered everywhere.

My heart is racing, my mind flying.

Is she armed?

My gun got taken off me when Grossman brought us in.

Do we need to be worried about her shooting at us? Am I about to die?

Julia doesn't seem to care. She doesn't slow down, sprinting with her torchlight held so steady it's like it's bolted onto a rail. I'm behind, barely keeping up as I trip over a barrel and stumble to catch my feet.

We're up a flight and she's cut away from the stairwell. Ahead, the girl is a glimpse of a shadow. She's like a whisper. I see her for a second in the next room, and then I don't. Julia doesn't slow down for a second, though, so I keep charging.

When Julia stops, it's so sudden I have to throw myself to the side to stop from barrelling into her.

I get my balance and look up, slowly swinging my torch across the room.

We've lost her, I realise.

She's gone.

A lump catches in my throat. She could be anywhere.

We're in another very large room—what I'm guessing is a storage room like the one downstairs, but this one is different. Julia's staring at the walls, and as I turn around, shining my torch to focus on where she's looking, I see they're covered in spray paint. Graffiti.

I move closer, focusing my light on one wall. There's more: photos that have been pasted there, documents and papers—laminated to keep them safe—all connected to one another by wire and red string like some giant conspiracy murder board. Bits and pieces of the painted text I recognise: names like Merkaton, Donaldson, Maragold, Handoler, Yegorov.

The whole wall is plastered with it. In the corner, Julia illuminates a small tent, and the beaten-down ashes of a makeshift fire. There's a table with trinkets on it, a single pistol, and a small chair. Beside that, a large duffel bag that looks full.

Julia's not saying a word. I can't even hear her breathing.

I take a few steps towards the bag to take a look inside, but there's a shout from Julia and her light goes out.

I spin back, torch swinging violently; I barely have time to register Julia's *"Look out!"* before the girl slams into my side.

I tumble, hitting the floor hard. You forget how heavy a human body is—even a small one like hers. But this is no street brawler knockdown. She's got her legs tight around my arms, pulling them back and back and back until my bones shriek in pain because they're not meant to bend that way. I try to scream, but her wrist is on my throat and her other arm is pulling into a chokehold.

I gasp for air, but there's nothing. My legs kick violently. My torch rolls across the floor, light dancing off the walls uselessly. I try to throw myself against her, use my weight to knock her into the ground, but each time I move she shifts, clambering about my body like a spider, like a parasite.

Her wrist tightens further. Dark spots flicker in my vision.

Then she yelps and releases me, falling off me and to the floor. I roll and grab my torch, flicking it upwards to see Julia kick her in the ribs, and then again in the head.

Blood splatters stone.

I want to get up and help, but I'm still gasping for oxygen.

Julia goes for another kick, but this time the girl's ready. She's fast—*insanely fast*—and is on her feet in between breaths. Julia lunges at her, hands out to grapple, but she slips out of the hold like she's made of smoke.

Julia hits the floor and grunts, winded, not getting up.

The girl darts past me and grabs the duffel bag.

She kicks the torch out of my hand, and it skitters across the floor before flickering off, sending us all into black.

By the time I find it and light the room up again, she's long gone, along with whatever was in that bag.

"She's gone," I croak, my throat red raw. "We lost."

Julia gets to her feet, picking up her own torch and flicking it on. "No, we didn't."

I try to push myself to my feet, and groan at the ache in my body. "It sure felt like we did."

"Why didn't she kill us?" Her breath is heavy and laboured. "It doesn't make any sense. She had the advantage over us in this building from the first second. We should either be dead, or we should never have found her."

I push myself to my feet. "What are you saying?"

Julia points her own torch at the walls, covered with the notes and the photos and the graffiti. "The attack at Paul's. The label. It was too easy. Those weren't mistakes. She wanted us to find this. She was sending us a message."

DCI John Grossman: I'd been driving around Islington for fifteen minutes and had pretty much given up. Here's the thing—fifteen minutes might not seem that long, but when you're tailing a suspect it might as well be an age of history. In fifteen minutes, anyone can get far enough away in any direction to never be caught up with again.

I was really kicking myself—I was tired, I figured. It had been a very long night and I'd been unlucky. Time to go back to the station and deal with Julia, and Mark, and whatever else was coming my way.

Then I saw it: Horner's car. I had to stop myself from slamming on the brakes and waking up the neighbourhood with tyres screeching. But it was definitely there—a black Mercedes with the right number plate, parked on a side street off the main road.

I pulled in round the corner and slipped out of the car slowly. I took the hoodie that I had in the back of my car and put it on, throwing the hood up so my face was covered. Instinctively, I took a pair of cuffs from the glove box and shoved them in my pocket. I didn't know if I was going to have to make an arrest tonight, but having them on me felt right.

I waited. The night was cool, the air fresh. I leant against a wall, got out my phone, and did my best to blend in with the scenery.

It worked and it didn't. I got a few worried glances. A young white couple coming stumbling out of a bar crossed the street when they saw me. An old man glanced back at me as he turned the corner. I wasn't invisible, but that didn't matter. I also knew that I wasn't a person to them. I wasn't an individual. You grow up in London, you learn that quickly. I was just a black man in a hoodie, and that told all the white people on this street all they needed to know about me. There would be no reason to look twice.

Ten minutes later, I saw Horner come out of a building down the road. It's strange—because it wasn't the sort of place I would ever imagine seeing a man like him. It had a sign that said LOW COST SAFE BOXES above, one of those places with PO boxes and safe boxes of different kinds—where you rent a small area in order to have your stuff kept out of sight and overseen by cameras and a twenty-four-hour concierge. It was where you kept things if you wanted them off record.

I watched Horner get back in his car and drive off, and all I can think is: *This is the first place he came after talking to Julia. He drove straight here. Whatever's inside, there's my answer.*

After waiting for Horner's car to be well out of sight, I dropped the hoodie back off in my own and swapped it out for a police badge.

And then . . . Okay, I guess I'm going to have to tell you. I reached into the glove compartment and I grabbed the closest piece of paper I could find—I think it was a letter from the council about tax—and folded it up a couple of times, sticking it in my pocket.

Now, I know that what I did next was not strictly legal. I can put my hands up and admit that. But let me try to provide some context: three people had just died, one of them an impossible meat-puppet of a clone. I had no real leads, my department was falling to pieces, and I was potentially going to face some kind of suspension in the morning. I needed *something*.

And, if I'm honest, being back out in the field had sent bolts of electricity crackling through my veins—I missed it. The chase, the stakeout, the leads. I was buzzing like I haven't done in ages.

If this is the worst thing I get done for, I can live with that. I think being honest at this point is probably more important.

So forgive me if I walk into Low Cost Safe Boxes with the full arm of the law, flashing my badge, and waving that folded letter in the concierge's face, saying, "Metropolitan Police. I have a warrant to access one of your safe boxes. The last man that came in here—Norman Horner—though he may well be trading under an assumed name."

The concierge, an old guy with a cleft lip and a scowl, shrugged at me. Getting up without a word, he led me to the right box. I suppressed a smile. He knew it was more than his job was worth to fight something like this. The safety of a box like this wasn't really in its security, but in its anonymity. Horner probably never expected it would be found.

After the concierge sat back down, I opened the box.

It was piled with beige folders, loads of them, each one labelled a different date. The dates moved slowly backwards through time as I went down. The folder on the top had the day before's date on it, and then there was one every three or four months previous going back what must have been five years.

I looked in the one on top—the most recent—and flicked through the pages. There were stock reports, indications of how the stock market had risen and fallen, with notes on where to buy and sell and how to short certain areas of the market.

Frowning, I noticed the dates at the top of the individual reports. May 2021, then June, August, September, going forward about six months into the future. Were these predictions, then?

There was nothing about possibility on them, though. The facts and figures were certain, as if they'd already happened.

I looked at another folder—one from about a year ago. It, too, had stock market details for the following six months, in exactly the same format as the future ones. Getting my phone out, I checked the details. They were all perfectly accurate, down to the decimal point.

That didn't make sense.

I looked back at the most current folder, rubbing my eyes. It was made to look as though someone had peeked into the future and written down exactly what would happen, every shift in the market, every trade, every deal. Why would someone fake that?

There was another folder at the bottom of the box that I hadn't noticed straightaway. This one was a different colour—a navy blue. There was no date on it.

Inside, a single page said: CONTAINMENT.

I flicked over the first page and my heart really started pounding.

Photos of dead bodies. Page upon page of them.

Underneath, each of them had two dates—*date of attempted breach* and *date of disposal*. They were all in the past, some from a few months ago, some from years before.

That's when I realised that I'm going to have to find Horner immediately. I'm going to have to go to his home and get to the bottom of this, procedure be damned.

Because the worst thing, the thing that really made my stomach turn?

I recognised all of them. Merkaton, Yegorov, Donaldson, Maragold, Handoler, Grodmann. These were people I knew. Half of them were *still alive*.

So why was I looking at all their dead bodies?

What the hell was going on?

Julia Torgrimsen: It was difficult to work out at first how it all linked together. Some of it seemed like nonsense—something out of a sci-fi film: there were pictures of a large box with a clock on it, labelled MACHINE #2. There were autopsy reports of what appeared to be bodies made entirely of muscle. There were dates from the far-off distant future, with notes about times and places that wouldn't happen for centuries.

But as Mark and I stood back to light up as much of the room as possible, one thing stood out really clearly.

Along one long flat stretch of wall, there was a countdown.

Or, rather, there was a single phrase that had been spray-painted in red and crossed out and replaced again and again and again.

5,354,832 years remaining.

But it was crossed out, replaced underneath with *4,349,253 years remaining.*

And then that had been crossed out too. Over and

over again, the number had been amended, replaced with a smaller one.

1,536,003 years remaining.

604,682 years remaining.

212,309 years remaining.

2,632 years remaining.

Until the very last one—the only one that hadn't been crossed out.

403 years remaining.

"Remaining until what?" Mark whispered.

I let my torch slide down to the bottom of the wall, where one clear word was spelled out in horrifying red capital letters, as if written in blood.

EXTINCTION.

DC Mark Cochrane: So there I am—staring at the numbers—and a kind of horror washes over me. I can't explain it. There's no logic behind it. I want to pull out my notebook to jot down what I'm looking at but I don't know what the numbers mean or what that terrible word is meant to imply. All I know is that in this dark abandoned claustrophobic fucking warehouse, I've never been so goddamn scared in my entire life.

"Mark," Julia says. She's already moved on. She's looking at another section of wall. I'm frozen. Paralysed. "Look."

I don't, at first. I can't. It was just too damn much, you know?

Julia continues anyway.

"It's her plan," she says. "Of people she's planning to

kill. There's a picture of Bruno here, and an × *2* written in the bottom right-hand corner. Then there's a picture of Paul. Both of them have their faces crossed out. They've been dealt with. There's a few other pictures before them, also crossed out, but none I recognise."

I tear myself away from the image, shining my light in her direction. She winces, putting up a hand to protect her eyes as I shine the torch right in her face.

"Are there any more? After Bruno and Paul? Are there any not crossed out yet?"

She nods. "There's one. Only one left. And my guess is that's where she's heading right now."

"*Who?*"

She swings her torch along the wall, illuminating the last photo—the pointed nose and sharklike grin of Norman Horner.

5

DC Mark Cochrane: So I'm absolutely shitting myself. I'm trying really hard not to show it, because—and I'm not ashamed to admit this—there's a big part of me that really wants Julia to be impressed by me, you know?

Maybe that's too much to hope for. She's barely said a word since we left that awful warehouse. My nose still trickles blood occasionally from where that girl broke it. My wet clothes are sticking to the seats and the stench still clogs my nostrils, but the only thing between me and my thoughts is a stretch of relatively empty road. It isn't helping.

The first hints of light touch the sky. Early commuters are out, hitting the roads before traffic picks up. I glance at the digital clock on the car's dashboard—on Kate's dashboard—and it says 5:12. I should be a zombie by now, but I've never felt so awake in my entire life.

Because, and I know this sounds ridiculous, I could have sworn that the pictures that I saw on that wall were pictures of *time travel*. I mean, actual *Back to the Future, Terminator*-style time travel, and I'm trying really hard to convince myself that this is all some absurd conspiracy made with deepfakes or something.

But I can't get that image out of my head—of a

countdown, getting closer and closer with every number being crossed out.

403 years remaining.

Somehow, it's worse than the crossed-out pictures of dead murder victims. It's worse than a violent and highly trained killer on the loose. It's worse because I *don't understand it.*

We pull onto Horner's road. Julia knew the address by heart. It's a busy part of town when it's not five in the morning—a bustling district of central London with a mixture of high-end flats and office space. Julia took the pistol that the girl left behind, but we were still back to only one weapon between the two of us.

That didn't feel like enough.

We roll up to a gate with a concierge behind a solid glass panel. He slides it down and asks us who we're visiting, without blinking an eye at the odd time of night—or day, I guess. Julia tells him and he closes his window, calling up to Horner to ask for permission. For a long moment, I think he's going to say no, that Julia's going to have to go extracurricular again, and I worry what that's going to look like, what new level of madness she can pull me into.

It doesn't occur to me that I might be able to refuse.

Not now.

I'm in too deep.

The concierge doesn't even slide open the glass panel again. The gate just opens. For a moment, I think about how this is the second time Julia's name has opened a locked door today. I don't have much time to consider this though, because she turns to me and says, "Welcome to the lion's den, Mark. When we go inside, don't say a word unless I tell you to. Not a single word."

Julia Torgrimsen: The last time I was in that building, it had been to see Anna. I couldn't help but think about it as we got to the lift, even with everything else going on. I thought I was done. I thought I was out, that I wouldn't have to be haunted by this anymore.

Maybe that's my punishment. Maybe I'm doomed to repeat all this, again and again and again, like some kind of sick purgatory, for the rest of time.

Mark must have sensed my tension, because he tensed up right next to me. The poor kid had become so reliant on my direction in all this that he was practically matching my breathing patterns.

It was then that I had an odd thought. I didn't like it. I didn't want it to be there, but somehow it had weaselled its way into my brain and it was staying put. Perhaps it was being back in Horner's building, and the memories of Anna, that brought it on.

In a way Mark was a lot like Anna had been—naive, idealistic, out of his depth. Realising that didn't make me feel comfortable at all.

We were headed up to the penthouse, where Horner lived, and I tried to focus back on the case at hand. I felt the weight of the shooter's pistol in my hand—a Zastava PPZ, Serbian, also with a suppressor. That and the Russian rifle got me thinking about organised crime connections in the Balkans, which then got me thinking about human trafficking, and about Anna all over again.

Before I knew what I was doing I quickly tapped the button for one of the floors on the way. The lift pulled to a stop and the doors opened.

"What's up?" Mark asked me.

"Nothing," I said. I stepped out into the corridor and fumbled in my pockets. "I need a cigarette."

He blinked at me. "Seriously? Now?"

I growled at him and he took a step back like I'd pulled a knife. I wasn't interested in explaining myself—what this place reminded me of. I needed a smoke and for the whole world to shut up for a second.

It felt like I'd barely taken a drag and the damn thing was already finished. I eyed my packet, considering lighting another one, but the sheer awkwardness of Mark standing there pointedly not looking at me was getting to be too much to bear.

When we got back in the lift, he didn't say another word. Maybe my warning to keep his mouth shut was on his mind.

Good, I thought. There were five million ways this could go south, and I didn't want Mark to be one of them.

The lift pinged when it hit the top floor.

Behind its doors was the very last thing I would have ever expected to see.

DCI John Grossman: Would you believe that I was actually stuck in traffic? In *traffic*, at half past five in the morning. Roadworks apparently, tons of them, and then some idiot crashed into the back of another right in the middle of a roundabout.

Part of me wanted to turn on the old blue and whites and zoom through London, but the truth was there wasn't any genuine urgency. Or at least, I didn't think there was. Sure—I needed to talk to Horner about those bodies, about those strange future stock market reports and dates. But I didn't have any evidence to suggest anyone's life was in immediate danger.

So I sat there, waiting.

DC Mark Cochrane: The place is an absolute state. I mean—it's clearly not always like this. It's a ridiculously fancy penthouse, spread over two floors, with all the rich ostentatious nonsense you'd expect to see in Hollywood films about billionaires. There's a TV so big it might as well be a cinema, and there's a bar—I mean, an actual full-length bar, like we're in a hotel—and there's a grand piano in the main living room. Can you call it a living room? I don't know. I don't feel like traditional room names apply to places like that.

It's not difficult to see how impressive it would look in normal circumstances, but right now it looks like a dump. There's papers everywhere. And I mean *everywhere*. They're strewn across the bar and over the tables. Some are on the floor and some stuck to the full-length glass windows. I think there'd be a pretty stunning view of London from up here if they weren't covered in paper.

I can't immediately see what's on them—they look like spreadsheets, or legal documentation of some kind. There are some pictures buried underneath the piles.

Then there's the clothes.

There's an open suitcase in the middle of the room and clothes are strewn all around it, as if Horner's packing to leave but he can't figure out what to take with him. The suitcase looks like it's been packed and unpacked about ten times.

"Going somewhere?" Julia asks, looking at the door in the corner of the room.

I turn to see Horner's silhouette standing in the doorway. He's holding a glass of whisky. His hair is dishevelled and his tie is loosened, dangling around his neck like a noose.

"Julia," he says. "So kind of you to visit. Care for a drink, dear?"

Julia Torgrimsen: I can't remember exactly what the word was—whether it was *darling,* or *honey,* or one of the other infantilising slurs that Bruno used to use—but the moment I heard it my entire body bristled. Over a decade of disgust and anger and hatred bubbled its way out of my stomach and right up into my head. I hadn't realised how much I'd been holding on to.

"What the fuck is going on, Norman?" I snapped. I took two steps towards him, and Mark must have picked up something in my manner because he looked like he was about to reach out and grab my arm.

A sharp look quickly disabused him of that idea.

I was about to grab Horner, strangle him, beat him until he told us everything, but he just leant back against the doorframe and sighed dramatically. "Just doing a little spring cleaning."

I paused. There was a casual ease to his manner that was utterly incongruous with the scene that surrounded us. The papers, the clothes, the mess. It screamed panic.

And yet, here he was, distinctly not panicked.

He had discovered something. Something had changed.

The contrast brought me back to my senses. He wasn't going to tell me anything unless he wanted to, and he didn't seem to be in the sharing mood.

Think, Julia.

"I know what's going on," I said. "I know about the girl. About the bodies."

It was a vain attempt. A stab in the dark to see if he'd open up.

"Oh, really?" Horner raised his eyebrows, taking a couple of steps into the room. He was swaying a little. "Do tell."

"I know about the time travel," I said, risking a few more specifics. "And the countdown. To extinction."

Mark's whole body tensed up behind me. I didn't need to see it. I could *feel* it.

Horner simply shrugged. "In which case, you know what's going to happen next. To be honest, Julia, I'm surprised you're still sober."

"She's coming to kill you, do you know that?"

"Oh, I don't see that it matters anymore." He sauntered his way over to the bar, brushing away a pile of papers. He leant down to find a half-empty bottle of Macallan 21, letting it slosh into his glass. "Not now containment's been broken. I thought I had such a handle on it—thought I knew what they were all doing with their jaunts into the future, but . . . I mean look at all this." He waved his hands at the scattered papers. "Just me trying to cling onto control. But there's no point now, is there?"

"What do you mean 'containment'?" Mark asked, and I swirled around in fury.

"What the fuck, Mark?"

He blinked, as if he had no idea what he did wrong. "What?"

Idiot.

"I told you not to speak."

"But I just—"

Horner laughed, like a delighted hyena. "Ah, but you see, *Mark,*" he goaded, layering more condescension into the name than I thought was humanly possible. "Julia here was probably going to attempt to ask something someone in the know would say, something like *'When did the containment break?'* or *'Can you be certain of the evidence?'* but thanks to you it's abundantly clear that neither of you has any idea what is going on. It's beautiful, really."

Mark grimaced, his face flushing red. "Well, you seem to have given up, anyway. So tell us: what is going on? The time travel? The clones? What the fuck is happening here?"

Horner shook his head and gave a wry smile. "Oh no, no. I'm not going to tell you. We may all be doomed, but at least if that spiteful little bitch does kill me, I'll have the satisfaction of seeing Julia's face knowing that she had no idea why. That almost makes it worth it."

A phone by the lift started ringing. Horner barely even registered it. He was leaning back on the bar, looking at his glass.

"That will be the guard at the front gate," I said.

Taking my prompt, Mark walked over and picked it up. "There's no one on the other end. The line is dead."

I swore. "Then the guard probably is too. She's here."

"What do we do?" Mark asked, his eyes wide in fear.

"We catch her," I replied. He blinked incredulously, as if I'd told him we're going to space. My gaze shifted from Mark, then over to Horner, and I realised that he wasn't going to be any help at all. Whatever had happened to him, he didn't seem to care if he lived or he died. Scanning the room, I let the beginnings of a plan come together in my head. "Okay. Listen closely: this is what we do."

DC Mark Cochrane: I'm crouched down behind the bar, trying to get a sense for the lay of the land. The main living space is open-plan—it runs from the lift, past the bar, to the floor-to-ceiling windows. On the far side, steps lead up to the next level. Underneath them, there's the door to a bedroom—Horner's bedroom, I assume—which we've left ajar. In the bed, covers over the top of him, is the curled-up lump of Norman Horner, passed out from too much drink.

Julia left the bottles out on the bar to prove it.

From where I am hidden, I have a direct line of sight to both the lift doors and the bedroom door. But there's no line between the bedroom and the lift. No sneaky rifle shots from the lift today. No, sir.

Julia has the gun. The issue is obvious: If it came down to a face-to-face matchup, which one of us would be more likely to freeze up? I'm not embarrassed to know that's me. No one should be embarrassed to say they'd freeze before taking someone else's life.

She's hiding behind the bedroom door—perfectly still like a statue. The scene is almost too perfect: Horner, in some state of panic about something that *he still won't tell us about*, got way too drunk and passed out in his bed. Easy target.

The door is just open enough so she can see where he would have gone, but just closed enough so she'll have to go in the room. When she does, Julia will subdue her, and I'll be right behind for backup. We've left music on—a bass-filled pump of electronic club music to cover the sound of my footsteps as I follow behind her. Sure, it'll cover her footsteps too, but I've got my phone in my hand with a text message ready to send to Julia. The moment her phone buzzes in her pocket, she'll know the girl is here. She'll be ready.

There's no reason this shouldn't work. That's what I kept telling myself. There's no reason anything should go wrong. We'll catch her and discover this whole time travel clone nonsense is a big hoax. We'll clear my and Julia's names, and later today I'll go back to Kate—apologise about the car thing—and we'll snuggle up on the sofa with the cat and watch *Indiana Jones*.

The lift door opens and my heart rises into my throat. She's holding the same rifle she used to kill Bruno. She's still wearing the same dust-stained hoodie. She's holding the same duffel bag she escaped with. She takes a step out of the lift, looking left and right, and I hold my breath.

DCI John Grossman: When I rolled up to the gate at Horner's building, there was something obviously wrong. The gate appeared to be closed at first, but as I stopped I realised that it had been pushed slightly ajar—just enough to fit someone through.

I had to lean over the steering wheel of my car a little to see where the guard was. There was no one behind the glass panel, which was odd for a building like that. People pay a lot of money to have security on hand 24/7.

As I was straining forward, I noticed a smudge of red at the bottom right corner of the glass and about thirty alarm bells started ringing in my head at the same time.

By the time I cut round to the door of the security hut, the adrenaline was racing through me. My hand was clenched around my Glock, and I was highly thankful I'd had the good sense to keep it on me when I was following Horner's car.

I pushed into the room with a thrust, quick-checking corners and desks.

It was empty, except for the guard.

He was on the floor, spread-eagled, with a knife sticking out of his eye.

Shit, was my first thought.

And before I had time to have a second one, I'd pushed

through the gate and was running full-tilt for the lift up to Horner's penthouse.

Julia Torgrimsen: I was waiting for the buzz of my phone against my leg to tell me she was approaching the door. I pulled the gun to my chest and strained my ears against the music, seeing if I could pick anything out.

Shoot her in the legs, I repeated in my head. *Incapacitate, but don't kill. We need her. We need to find out what's happening here.*

After what felt like a lifetime, I was starting to think she wasn't coming. Mark hadn't messaged me yet. And surely, she'd have come in by now? How long had passed—two minutes? Three?

DC Mark Cochrane: For the longest time, she just stands there—about three steps in front of the lift—and she doesn't move. It's like she's fallen into a standing coma, or something, except her eyes are shifting left and right, taking in every facet of the room.

I duck back down, making sure she doesn't see me, making sure I don't make a single sound.

I think about sending the text, but she hasn't started walking towards the room yet. That wasn't in the plan and I don't want to do something stupid. Why isn't she taking the bait? What is she waiting for?

Then, slowly, like someone's playing a video recording at half-speed, she puts down the duffel bag, and she moves.

She walks towards me.

I pull myself tight under the bar and out of sight, my

heart pounding. I'm holding my breath and I feel like it's going to burst out of me in one big exhalation.

I can't see where she is anymore. I can't even hear her.

There's a click and the room goes silent. She's turned off the music.

I hear a light footstep, and another moving away from me. I dip my head from around the bar, and see her walking, slowly, cautiously, towards the door to the bedroom where Horner's sleeping mound lies.

She's barely making a sound, like she's gliding on ice, but she's definitely moving.

I can't follow anymore. She'll hear me behind her. It's just her and Julia until I can catch up with them.

I'd send the text, but I'm worried she'll hear the buzzing of Julia's phone now the music's gone. I hope that the music cutting out is itself enough of an indication.

Three paces. Four. Five.

All she has to do is walk through that door and Julia will take her down.

She's only about two metres away from the bedroom door when the lift opens again with a loud *ping*.

She spins, raising her rifle, quick as lightning.

The door opens on Grossman—*fucking Grossman*—holding a pistol.

"*No!*" I shout, diving out from behind the bar.

But it's too late. She fires twice and he doubles over, falling to the ground.

Julia Torgrimsen: I was such a bundle of energy and tension, like a taut bowstring straining at its very edge, that when I heard Mark shout I exploded forward.

Slamming the door out of the way, I burst into the main room to find chaos.

Mark running. John down.

Wait, John? I thought. *What the fuck is he doing here?*

But I didn't have time to wonder. The girl, a metre or so in front of me, was tracking Mark with her rifle, about to shoot him too.

There wouldn't even be enough time to get my gun up.

I shouted—not a word, just a harsh bellow of sound—and she spun.

My gun came up, but her rifle knocked it as I pulled the trigger, sending the bullet wide.

I'd only just processed the idea of tackling her when she undercut my legs with a capoeira-style swoop and sent me tumbling to the floor. The pistol fell out of my hand, skittering behind me.

She straightened with her rifle, pointing it at my face.

She stopped. She could have pulled the trigger. She had time. I knew it.

But she didn't. She frowned at me, as if trying to decide what she should do.

Then Mark barrelled into her at full speed and they both went tumbling into the bedroom.

DC Mark Cochrane: *Not again,* I think, as we land on the floor. *Why do I always end up in a wrestling match with her?*

It goes about as well as you'd expect.

I try to pin her arms down, get them behind her back.

She headbutts me in the nose—my already fucking broken nose—and it's all I can do not to pass out. Pain screams across my forehead. Blood spills out of my face, all over her.

My grip loosens on her arms just enough for her to slip free. I'm on my knees, gasping, gurgling on my own blood as it drips into my throat. I try to grapple her torso, to hold her down.

Her knee slams straight into my balls.

That's me done.

I'm out.

My head swimming, I fall backwards. My eyes have dark spots in them, blinking in and out. I roll over in time to see her lift her rifle, point it at the figure on the bed, and fire three times. Feathers explode into the air.

She tugs back the covers to reveal a pile of pillows in the shape of a human body.

She turns back to look at me, furious, and I'm certain she's going to kill me this time.

This is it. This is how I die.

Then there's a buzz of electricity, and she jerks. Her muscles jitter and shake, convulsing, and she collapses on the floor in a heap.

Horner steps into the room, a drink in one hand and a Taser in the other.

"Well," he says, sardonically. "That went well."

6

DCI John Grossman: I'd taken two shots the second I stepped out of the lift. The impact had doubled me over, like being punched in the gut, but once I was over the shock, the main sensation was just pain. It felt like my stomach was on fire, being seared over a hot grill. I had to breathe long and hard to stay conscious, to work out what the hell was going on.

For a short while, all I could focus on was the blood seeping through my clutching hands and onto the floor. *Is that a lot of blood?* I thought. *How much is too much? I can probably stand to lose a little.*

That's where my brain was at, rationally—focusing on the little things to get through the moment, to get through the pain.

And when I looked up, guess who was standing right in front of me.

Yep—you guessed it.

Julia.

Fucking Julia.

"What are you doing here?" she demanded.

"What am *I* doing here?" I managed. "What the hell are *you* doing here? You're . . . supposed to be back at the station, *under arrest*. I told that idiot Mark to . . ." I glanced behind her and saw Mark crawling out of the bedroom door, blood pouring down his face. "Oh Jesus Christ, *seriously?*"

"Calm down, John," Julia said, crouching next to me. "You're losing a lot of blood."

Oh, I thought. *So it is a lot.*

Julia looked a little hazy, like someone had put a veil over her. I remember thinking: *God, she really does look like shit.*

And, I think, that's when I passed out.

DC Mark Cochrane: As soon as the girl's down, Julia goes straight to Grossman. I don't hear what they say, but she seems worried. He must have blacked out, because he's lolling back in her arms as she rips off some of his clothes and uses it to stymie the wound and try to slow the bleeding.

I pull myself to my feet, lifting my own sleeve to my bloody nose. I wince as it touches it—the sting running down my whole body. I'm still nauseous from the kick in the balls. I feel like I'm going to throw up.

"I'll call an ambulance," I mutter.

"Don't." Julia turns round. She kneels down beside him and opens his shirt, checking over his body. She's made a makeshift dressing for the wound on his stomach. "He'll live," she said eventually. "He got lucky. One of the bullets bounced off his belt buckle, and there's only one entry wound. No vital organs."

I stare at her. "He's *unconscious*."

"It's the blood," she says, shaking her head. "For a detective, John's never been very good with blood. The moment an ambulance gets here, so do the rest of the police, and we'll have lost our chance to question her."

I look back at the girl on the floor. She's out cold too. Horner is standing over her like a vulture assessing a corpse for scraps. He takes a sip of his whisky.

"The decoy was a good idea," he says. Then slowly, almost casually, he reaches down and picks up the gun she dropped. "We should kill her while she's out."

"*What?*" I say, but Julia's already on her feet.

Julia Torgrimsen: It was a collection of things—his tipsy nonchalance, that slimy half grin on his face, the casual suggestion of murder—together, they reached down deep inside of me and tripped off something that I'd kept buried for a very long time. A Pandora's box of hatred, of fury, of self-loathing—it cracked right open. There was nothing I could do about it. I think I might have hit him a couple of times.

DC Mark Cochrane: "Hit him a couple of times"? Is *that* what Julia said? No, no. Let me tell you what happened.

She storms right past me, not even glancing at me. The thing is, even if I wanted to, I wouldn't have stepped in her way. It was like—I remember I went on this holiday to the Philippines back in '09 with Kate, when we were still doing the whole backpacker thing, and one night the highest typhoon-level alert was called—like, a proper category 5 hurricane. I remember looking at the sea outside the hostel we were staying in, seeing the waters swell and the clouds darken like it was night. There was this sense of inevitability—of the fury of nature. There was no choice, nothing that could be done. We had to batten down the hatches, stay inside, and pray that it was over soon.

I would have sprinted into that hurricane naked rather than stepping in front of Julia at that moment.

Horner's still looking at the gun in his hand when she kicks it and it goes flying across the room. He half-turns, a little slow from the drink, and her elbow takes him hard in the mouth. His head jerks back, spluttering.

She doesn't stop. She falls on him, fists and limbs flying. His yelps and cries are staccato, punctuated with every punch and kick to his stomach, his face, his chest.

Jesus Christ, I think, just standing and staring. *She's beating the shit out of him.*

When she's done, he's barely conscious. He's muttering something through his bloody lips, but I can't make out what it is. Julia's fists are covered in blood, her arms are splattered up to the elbows.

She grabs him by the hair—the fucking *hair*—and pulls him across the room to a metal railing at the far side.

"Cuffs," she says, and holds her hand out to me without looking at me.

I oblige. She cuffs a whimpering Horner to the railing and then turns back to me.

"Wake her up," she says. "It's time we found out what the hell is going on."

Julia Torgrimsen: John was going to be okay. Once the bleeding clotted, he'd even be able to move around. He'd need medical attention soon, sure, but it was nothing that couldn't wait. There were more important issues at hand.

We propped the girl into a chair and she was already starting to stir. Fortunately John had another pair of cuffs in his pocket, so Mark and I had her arms held tight behind her back.

When her eyes opened, she surveyed the scene. John down. Mark bleeding, and still panting. And then finally her eyes landed on Horner, half-awake and bloody. A smile appeared on her face.

"I knew leading you two here was the right idea." Her accent was light, but definitive. Eastern European. Her voice was steady. "I wasn't sure you'd taken the bait."

"Who are you?" I asked.

"I've been using Lilja for . . . a while. Let's go with that."

Given what had happened, and where she was, she seemed surprisingly relaxed. But I've been in enough interrogations. Underneath her confident veneer there was something else she was struggling to keep in. Fear. She might have been a good killer, but she wasn't as good of an actor as she thought she was.

"Why did you kill them? Bruno, Paul, the others. Why were you planning on killing Horner?"

Her lips turned up into a scowl. "Because they deserved it."

"Why?"

She laughed. "*Why?* You, of all people, ask *why*? I know who you are, Julia Torgrimsen. I know what you did. You know they deserve it more than anyone."

I shook my head. This wasn't getting me anywhere.

This was more than a revenge spree—there had been something so systematic about her movements, about her plans in that warehouse. "What about the countdown?"

She looked at me for a long moment, and her eyes went hard as steel. "You won't believe me. That's why I brought you here, Julia. That's why I set this up, to pull you back in. You have to see it for yourself."

I kept my breath steady, but I could feel my heart in my chest. What did she mean, *that's why I set this up*?

"See what?"

"The great machine of our doom. The greatest invention of our time. The last thing humanity will ever create."

"What the hell are you talking about?" Mark demanded, taking a step forward. His twisted nose made his voice sound nasal and squeaky.

"A time machine," I said.

Her lips tightened into a thin line. "My father's greatest invention. And his worst."

I blinked. *My father.* Pieces began to fall into place.

"Who was your father?"

"Ivan Jukić," she replied, with a sad little smile. "One of the best Bosnian scientists before the war. We came to this country in '99, fleeing the conflict when I was just an infant."

I suppressed a small gulp. She was almost exactly the age Anna would have been if she were still alive.

"So your father invented a time machine? Why? How did he get involved with"—I gestured around me—"these people? I worked with them for years. Why have I never heard of him, or of you?"

"It was Bruno Donaldson that picked him up first, intrigued by his promises. My father just wanted to fix things—the war, the mistakes. When they realised what he could do, more got involved. They started paying him a lot of money."

"To travel into the past?"

"No—the future."

Behind me, I heard Mark scoff. He was standing there with that infuriating notebook of his, looking like an idiot. "That's impossible."

She shrugged. "I'm no scientist, and I don't share my father's intellect. He always kept me out of it. After what he had seen, he was obsessed with protecting me. He trained me from a young age to be ready for when people would turn on him and his invention. He knew they would come for him, for both of us." She paused, taking a breath. "He was not naive about the realities of our situation."

"Tell me more about his invention."

"I don't know how it works, but the outcome is pretty simple: it lets you travel to the future. It didn't take long for Bruno and the others to realise what this meant for them: control of the market, the ability to buy or short stocks moments before things happened, being able to profit off disasters before they took place—nine-eleven, Fukushima, the tsunami in 2004."

"They made money?"

She laughed. "They made *so much* money. There's a group of them—a cabal of billionaires. They use the machine to make sure that every financial decision they make is the right one. To stay in control. Why do you think the wealth gap keeps growing? Luck? Hard work? No—they own the future. It belongs to them."

"This is ridiculous," Mark muttered from behind me. He was pacing.

"The truth is my father didn't really care about all that," Lilja continued. "He needed their funding. He hoped he might be able to prevent future wars, future disasters. He thought that if he could get in front of them, but . . ." She trailed off.

Old pain blossomed in my chest. This story was too familiar. "But they got greedy. They always do."

"It was Gabriel Maragold who was the first to push the boundaries. The near future wasn't enough. He wanted to go further, see how far forward he could go. My father warned him against it—said we didn't know what we'd find. But it was out of his hands."

"How far did they go?"

"A hundred years. Then a thousand. Then ten thousand. They kept pushing. I never saw it, but the things they described—giant megacities, space travel, you name it. Then further, millions of years. The world looked nothing like it did now. Humanity had colonised the solar system, the stars. Maragold wanted to see what he could steal from those futures, what he could bring back and profit off of. Then they went too far."

"Too far?"

She shook her head solemnly, looking down at the ground. "Six million years into the future. I remember it clearly. It was posted up on my father's wall for weeks. The extremity. The termination limit. My father went too far one day and he came back different."

"Different?"

"Whatever he saw, it sent him mad. He became obsessive, stopped sleeping, no longer made sense. A few weeks later, he . . ." She shook her head, as if disappointed. "He killed himself."

I got closer to her, inches from her face. I needed to understand. "What do you mean *the extremity*? Is this about the clones? Did he make those too?"

"I can't tell you," she whispered. "You won't believe me. But if you let me, I can show it to you. Then everything will be clear. The machine is here. Well, one of them is. In this penthouse. Norman keeps one for himself."

For a moment, a silence settled between us. It thrummed in the room, like a single note of tension.

"Show me," I said, and reached down to uncuff her.

DC Mark Cochrane: "Wait just a fucking second," I say, tucking my notebook into my jacket as Julia reaches to undo her cuffs. "What the hell are you doing?"

Julia doesn't even register me. She gets out the key and lifts it to the lock. And I think: I can't do this. I can't stand by and let this crazy serial killer be set free because she's made up some clearly insane story. I grab the gun from Julia's waist and point it at her.

"Stop that right now."

She looks at me and raises her eyebrows. "What are you doing, Mark?"

"I'm the cop here," I say. "You're not even police anymore. You're a . . . you're an *advisor*. She just shot

Grossman! You can't let her go after we've just got her. That's crazy."

And you know what Julia does? She completely fucking ignores me. I watch—helplessly—as she unlocks the cuffs and lets them fall to the floor. I mean, what am I supposed to do? Shoot her? Jesus Christ.

Lilja stands up and I take a few steps back, shifting the weapon onto her. My whole body is tense, expecting her to launch at me again.

She doesn't. She gets up, without a hint of a threat in her stance.

Pointing at her rifle, still on the floor from where I tackled her, she says to Julia, "Pick that up. You're going to need it."

Leading the way, followed by me with the pistol and Julia with a rifle, she makes her way up the stairs and through the back of the room. She knows this place, like she knew Paul's house. She's been here many times before.

We pass through another living space on the second floor, but this is decked out as an office: bookcases, files, computers. There's a coffee machine in the corner. Like downstairs, it's a mess of strewn paper. She walks right past it and towards one of the bookcases at the back wall. Reaching up, she feels along the wooden side of the bookcase.

There's a click as she pulls something, and a creak, and the whole bookcase opens like a door.

Fuck me, I think. *Here we go. Into the Batcave.*

The room inside is small and clinical—white walls and

fluorescent light dominate. In the centre, there's a large grey machine that looks like something out of a sci-fi flick, like *Stargate,* or something. It's this tall, rectangular monolith, about eight feet high, and in the centre is what looks like a double door, though there's nothing on the other side. There were pictures of it in the warehouse.

On a screen at the top, there's a single number: 403.

403 years remaining, the graffiti in the warehouse had said.

She turns to us.

"The only way to understand is to see it for yourself. I didn't believe until I did. But there are rules, and you must promise me you'll follow them."

I glance at Julia, who's looking at her intently, then back at Lilja. I'm trying to work out why it feels like the girl who we had in cuffs is now giving us orders.

"I'm going in too," I say.

Lilja shakes her head. "No. Only her."

I point the gun at her again. "Listen to me. You're not the one in charge here. Okay, so maybe I wasn't going to shoot Julia earlier, but don't think for a second that I won't shoot *you* if I think there's something off here. I don't trust you for a second. If Julia's going, I'm going too."

She looks at me long and hard, and then lets out an exasperated sigh. "Fine. I'll give you a button to get out, *both of you*—press it and it'll bring you right back. Don't stay too long. A minute or two at most. Longer than that, and you'll start to see them."

"Who?" Julia asks.

"Them. It's hard to explain without being in it. We

don't really know what they are, or what they want. But they'll look like you. They'll sound like you. They'll act in every possible way like you. They'll beg you to take them back with you. They'll say anything. If you see one, don't listen to them. Don't even let them talk. The second you see one of them, kill them. That's why you're going in armed. They won't be armed—not at first."

I'm shaking my head, trying to get my head round these bizarre instructions. "What the hell are you on about?"

Lilja doesn't even glance at me. All her energy is directed at Julia.

"If you see one before you come out, you have to kill it before you leave. That's the first rule. The one everyone has to follow. Do you understand? Don't leave one alive if it's seen you. That's paramount."

Julia nods, as if she has any fucking clue what's going on, but how could she, because I sure as hell don't.

"But if you're only there a minute you should be fine. Don't spend long."

She walks over to the machine and presses a button on its side. She fiddles with some controls and then there's a loud beeping, like a truck reversing.

Lilja puts a small device in each of our hands with a single button.

"Use this to get out," she says, then backs away, stepping behind the machine.

The line down the middle of it—the one that looks like the crack in a doorway—begins to glow and then opens, and before I have a second to express how insane of an idea this all is, and how maybe we shouldn't be doing this, the whole room is engulfed in blinding light.

And I know this is going to sound utterly batshit insane, but when I open my eyes again, we're somewhere completely new.

It's swelteringly hot—the sun beats down furiously upon us and I can already feel my entire body sweating, desperate to get out of these clothes. I blink at the glare, staring around me at what appears to be . . . emptiness.

The landscape is utterly desolate, as far as the eye can see. The ground is blackened like it's been burnt and there's not a single living thing in sight except for Julia, next to me. The sky is cloudless, but instead of blue it is a deep bloodred. The air is thick and acrid in my throat, and I cough.

"What the fuck?" I manage. I quickly look at the device in my hand, my way home, feeling suddenly desperate to know where it is—this anchor, this lifeline. "What is this place?"

"Death," Julia says. "There is nothing here but death."

And she is right. It is the most lifeless scene I have ever encountered. Off in the distance, I think I might be able to see the remnants of buildings, but those too are blackened. I don't need to look any closer to know they are abandoned.

Nothing could possibly live here.

Or so I think.

I don't know how long we stand there staring at it, but it's clearly too long.

There's a scratching behind us. A rustle against the ground.

I spin around, frantic, unsure if I want to press the button or raise my weapon.

My chest tightens in panic when I see it.

Some twenty metres ahead of us, somehow impossibly risen out of the blackened nothingness, is Julia. Another Julia.

She is naked—there isn't a single piece of clothing, or anything inanimate on her—but she is undoubtedly Julia, in that moment. She is exactly the same.

I look at Julia and see her shudder, like she's seen a spider. Her breathing is shallow. I've never seen her shaken like this before, but I get it. The sight of it—the two Julias—makes me feel sick.

"Please," the new Julia whispers, holding out her hand. She starts to walk towards us, slowly, awkwardly, like she's just learnt how to do it. "Please. Help me."

And my sickness and horror morphs into something else, into a sudden desire to help her—this naked, pathetic woman in the middle of this devastation. Every instinct I have pushes me to go to her, to give her my jacket to cover herself with. To bring her back.

"Please," she says again, moving closer.

I lift up my arm to reach out for her, to offer her a hand, when Julia lifts her rifle and shoots her right in the chest.

I jerk backwards as her blood explodes out of her back and she flops to the floor.

"Jesus! What the fuck?!"

"The second you see one of them, kill them," Julia says quietly, her voice shaking. "Those were the rules."

"But she was helpless!" I shout back. "She was—"

"We have no idea what she was," Julia cuts back. "We need to get out of here. Now. Press your button."

She lifts her device and presses and, before I can blink, she's gone. No puff of smoke, no blinding light. She's just gone—like she's been edited out of the frame.

I reach for my device, but I fumble and drop it.

"Fuck." As I crouch down to pick it up, I hear another voice behind me.

Not just any voice.

My voice.

"Mark," it says. I turn around and there I am. *Me.* Exactly fucking me. Naked as the day I was born. He's even got a broken nose. "Mark—I need you to do exactly what I tell you if you want to live."

His voice is different from the other—clearer, more authoritative. He's about twenty metres away from me and walking closer, gradually closing the distance between us. I lift my pistol and point it right at him, heart pounding, head screaming.

"Stay back!"

He stops. "It's okay, Mark. I know what you're going through. I can fix all of this."

I hold my pistol directly pointed at him and finger the trigger. I should kill him—that's what Julia did. I should shoot him a bunch of times then press the button and get the fuck out of here.

I glance back and look at the dead, naked Julia on the ground behind me and I almost throw up.

Oh God. Oh God fuck fuck fuck.

"Don't do it, Mark," the thing says. *I* say. "Don't even think about it."

I hold my breath, about to close my eyes and shoot.

But I can't.

I can't fucking do it.

I can't shoot *myself*.

Jesus.

Hands shaking, I press the button.

In a blink, I'm suddenly back in that room.

It's just me, and Julia, and Lilja.

They're both looking at me.

"What happened?" Lilja asks. "Did you see one?"

"I . . ." I look at the gun in my hands. "No," I say. "No, I didn't see anything. Just . . . Just Julia, the *other* Julia, and then she left and . . . and I followed." I slump to the floor, shaking my head. "I didn't see anything."

"Good," she replies. "Because if you had and you hadn't killed it, I'd have had to kill you."

Julia Torgrimsen: Mark was an absolute fucking mess. I should have been too, but somehow I wasn't. There was something about what I'd seen—the madness of it, the impossibility—that pulled together threads in my head in a sudden rush of adrenaline. The two bodies of Bruno. The countdown.

This was the thing that tied it all together.

I looked up at the screen above the once again inert machine, and noticed the number had dropped.

399.

"What was that? How far forward did we go?" I ask Lilja.

She grits her teeth. "That was here, four hundred and three years in the future. That is the future of the planet and the human race. You want to know what that is, Julia? That is our extinction."

7

DC Mark Cochrane: I can't stop thinking about that place—the blackened ground, like the earth had been burnt to a cinder; the endless lifeless desolation; those *things*.

I think they were talking about something, but I could barely focus, you know? Every time I grasp onto a fragment of a sentence it gets truncated by one of my thoughts—*You lied to them, Mark. You didn't kill that thing.*

But it's not here—it's been left behind, inside that machine. *It'll be okay,* I told myself. *Get ahold of yourself. It'll all be okay.*

Julia Torgrimsen: I made her tell me everything. We'd left the room with the machine—Mark couldn't stand to be in it—and we ended up back in the living room. There were two big sofas but no one was sitting on either of them. Mark was pacing back and forth. Lilja and I were standing opposite each other, bolt upright like we'd been jolted with electricity.

Lilja walked to the large floor-to-ceiling windows and waved out at the city below us, bustling and thriving now with the morning rush hour. "Our guess? At some point in the future, about six million years in the future, humanity pushes too far out into the galaxy. It encounters *something*, another race of beings, another consciousness? Who knows? There's no trying to understand it. All we can understand is the consequence."

I took a deep breath. "Extinction."

"I don't know what we do, as a species. Maybe we don't do anything at all. Maybe it was always going to happen. But that's what my father saw: every last piece of humanity, every last human, gone. He called it the extremity."

"How?"

"We don't know. It's just wasteland. All we know about the extremity are the clones."

"Jesus Christ," Mark said. He was still pacing, looking at his hands, at the floor. "Jesus fucking Christ."

"It's not just that it looks like you," Lilja continued, ignoring him. "It *is* you. It's like a perfect copy of you in the moment that you are replicated. You can go into the future, but anyone who goes all the way to the extremity gets copied. It has all your memories, all your hopes and your fears and your desires. It knows you perfectly."

"What do they want?"

"We're still not sure. At the beginning, they brought one back, thought they could learn from it. Turns out they get stronger the longer you leave them alive. Smarter. By the time we realised what it was doing, it had killed twenty-three people."

I leant forward. "What *was* it doing?"

"It seems like they want the time machine, to take the technology for themselves. Our guess is that they don't have one, or they need ours for some reason, maybe to get more of them back here, to our timeline. And given where they come from, that can't be good. Can you imagine if one got control of the machine itself? How many more it could bring through?"

I shook my head. "But wait—we just went forward four hundred and three years, not six million."

"You're right. It took us a while before we discovered that anomaly. After my father stumbled upon the extremity, he made everyone agree not to go anywhere near it, so it was a while before we realised what was happening."

"What?"

"Each time we used the machine, every single time, the extremity moved closer. We don't know why. My father had theories, during his brief final moments of lucidity—he posited that the energy it created was like a beacon in time they could use to track us, and with each use they could zero in closer and closer. He built the timer, something that could probe into the future and identify where the cutoff was, and it just kept moving back."

I stared at her, baffled. "And they *kept using it*?"

She nodded. "At first, they pretended they didn't believe my father's theory. They said there wasn't enough evidence. Then they asked pet scientists to come up with ways to disprove it, and they clung onto every morsel. Confirmation bias is a powerful drug. Then, when all evidence of it was utterly undeniable, they came up with new arguments. It was so far away, they said, that eventually we would find some way to reverse it. That we'd be able to stop it before it got to us. And as it kept getting closer and closer, and their denial kept getting stronger and stronger, one thing was made utterly clear—they just didn't care.

"Giving up the machine meant giving up their profits. Their power. Their control. The actual burgeoning extinction of the human race didn't factor into that for them personally, since as long as it wasn't in their lifetime, then it didn't matter. Maybe when it was eighty years away, they'd stop. Or sixty. Maybe."

"Bastards," I muttered.

"Yes," she replied. "My father was working on a way to stop them, to destroy the machines, before he . . . before he died. I went underground after that. I've been working on it ever since."

She stopped talking, and the weight of her silence told me everything I needed to know.

"So why resurface now? You have a plan?"

She nodded, her face impassive. "I do, but things got brought forward. They started getting reckless—maybe it was the ticking countdown, maybe it was just greed. At first, Horner had a strict containment policy, clear protocols: secret passcodes, only working in pairs, that kind of thing. Then it was an outright ban on travelling to the extremity. But Bruno's clone in our timeline shows that people weren't following that. We've been breached—who knows how many times. So I killed Bruno. Fuck knows what he was after travelling out there, but frankly I don't care. Nothing will change their attitude. Nothing will make them stop playing God. So I'm going to kill them all and shut down these machines for good."

I frowned. Something wasn't right. "But . . . wait, we *just* went in. You made us go in, and the clock went back. We just brought the extinction forward. Why?"

She sighed. "There was no other way to convince you. To make you truly believe. I always knew I'd have to sacrifice a few years. In the face of maybe stopping it for good, it felt like a worthy sacrifice to make."

"What do you mean—you always knew?"

"You may not have known me, Julia, but I know you. You are a legend in these circles—the woman that killed Yegorov, that almost took down the group. I knew that if anyone was going to help me with this, it would be you. I've studied you, read about you. I set up that crime scene specifically so they would call you back in, so you wouldn't be able to resist."

"You moved the body. You left the clues. You wanted to be found."

She smiled. "Easy when you're the shooter. Get in before the police do, wear the right outfit, flash the right badge. You can clear a room and people will let you do anything."

"Why? Why not just . . . call me?"

Lilja laughed. "I tried. You don't have a phone number. You don't check your email. I wrote to you, Julia. I wrote you *thirty-seven letters*. You didn't read a single one. I even risked showing up at your door, knowing that they would be watching for me. You didn't answer—either drunk or asleep, or both. I needed something to *wake you up*."

I shook my head, trying to process this revelation. "But

why do you need me? You got this far on your own—why don't you destroy this machine now, right here?"

"Because it's not the only one."

Mark's head snapped round.

"There are *three of them*," she said. "But the other two are locked up so tight I can't get to them. The only way to find them is to go back to a moment in the past where they aren't so locked up, where I know they are in transit, and destroy them."

"Wait," Mark said, storming over to Lilja, jabbing a finger at her chest. "You want us to use that thing again? On purpose?"

She looked up at him, unshakable. "It's the only way."

"Jesus." He put his hand on his head. "Jesus Christ, this is madness."

I stepped in front of him. "I still don't understand. Why not travel twice—get to both machines yourself?"

"Because that's not how the machine works," Lilja replied. "It's designed for future-travel. I'll be reversing it, but it's not calibrated properly for that. My father could probably do it. But . . ." She trailed off, shaking her head. "From what I understand, my guess is it'll work *once*, then probably break. I think we've only got one shot, so I needed two people to be certain. One of us goes after one machine, one of us goes after the other at the same time. The only way to stop anyone using them, to stop the date moving even closer, is to destroy all three."

I looked up at the ceiling, trying to process this information. Already my head was sorting through the pieces like a detective—as if that's still what I was—

trying to work out the kinks, see the solutions. But there was a much larger issue at hand, one that was blaring behind it all.

"I don't want to believe it," I whispered. "I don't want to believe that the entire world is going to end."

Lilja shrugged. "You've seen it. You've already seen one of those things, and the only reason you managed to kill it was because it was just freshly made. The *simulacrum*, my father called them. They're real. They exist. And if we don't do something about these machines, one day one of the clones is going to get their hands on one and we'll be overrun."

"Two," Mark said. He was sitting down on the sofa. I hadn't seen him sit down. "There were two."

"*What?*" Lilja asked.

Mark let out a sigh that seemed to empty the life right out of him. "I lied."

DC Mark Cochrane: I'm trying to get my mind off that horrific place, trying to tell myself it'll all be okay, but everywhere I look there's a reminder of the horror—Grossman lying unconscious on the floor; Horner, bloody and beaten, cuffed to the radiator in the bedroom; and that *girl*, just talking. Talking and talking and talking and every word she says makes this whole situation worse.

Because as she speaks, it becomes abundantly clear.

The world is going to end.

It's all over.

Everything. Cats. Ice cream. Tacos. Sex. Going to the fucking cinema. It's *all* going to end in a few hundred years.

Just because some billionaire narcissists were too greedy and self-involved to stop and do the right thing.

And that's when the thought hits me—or at least, it had been hitting me for a while, but I'd been trying really hard not to acknowledge it—*That's me. I'm like them.*

That's what I'm doing right now. Lying about not seeing one of those things when I did, ignoring the consequences because I'm too goddamn scared of what will happen if I speak it out loud.

But I can't hold it in. Not after hearing that. Not knowing what I know.

And that's when I knew I had to speak up.

I didn't want to be one of those assholes. Not now. Not ever.

Julia Torgrimsen: Lilja's whole body tensed up, like a cobra about to strike. Mark's head was in his hands, covering his face, but I didn't need to see his eyes to realise he was crying. He was a mess, and Lilja looked like she was about to kill him.

"Wait," I said, stepping in between them. I lifted my gun up, ever so slightly. Enough to remind her it was there. "Let him explain."

Her eyes squinted, her brows furrowing together into tight lines, but she didn't move. She said nothing.

"Mark?"

Slowly, he tilted his head up. His eyes were red and haunted. "There was another. After you left, there was one of *me*. And I didn't kill him. I couldn't. I freaked out and came right back."

"Fuck!" Lilja shouted so loudly I almost stumbled. It's

the most emotion I'd seen from her yet. "God fucking damn it! I should never have sent him in. I sent *you* in because I trusted you. I know your record. I know your capabilities. I knew you wouldn't fuck up like this, but when I roped you into this I didn't realise that this idiot would be part of the package!"

Mark let out a low moan, putting his head back into his hands.

"What's the issue? So there's a simulacrum of Mark four hundred years in the future. Isn't it stuck there?"

She shook her head. "You don't understand! They latch onto the people they copy. Why do you think I killed Bruno and Paul? They can *follow*. Which is why we kill them immediately. But . . ." She waved her hands at the mess around her. "The whole reason Horner's gone insane is because once you lose a handle on one of them, they . . . Fuck!"

She reached over to grab the rifle off me.

"Wait!" I said, pulling back.

"He has to die, Julia. He has to. It's the only way."

"Stop!" I shout, wresting the gun away. "Talk to me first. What does this mean for us? It's coming here—to this moment in time?"

She took three deep breaths. "He's like an anchor—as long as that idiot exists in this timeline, it can follow him back through the machine if we use it again. But we *have* to use it again, because that's how we destroy the other ones! Which means the next time we use that machine to go somewhere—*anywhere*—Mark number two will be waiting there for us. And it will be ready this time. It won't be vulnerable like before." She took a step around me and raised her rifle again. "I'm sorry. It's the only way."

"No," I said. "You kill him and I'm out. I'm not helping you. And you can't do this alone, you've already said that."

"The *extinction of the human race*, Julia! You're putting humanity in jeopardy for *him*?"

I looked at Mark, whose face I still couldn't see because it was buried in his hands.

"Yes," I said, and then, and I couldn't believe I was saying it, "he can help us."

She looked at me for a hard second, then over at Mark, then stormed off to the other side of the room, muttering angrily to herself in a language I didn't understand.

"I'm sorry," Mark whispered. "I've fucked everything up. I always fuck everything up."

I sighed, taking a seat next to him. There would be a way to work this out, I knew there would. There was always a way out, but I needed Mark to get his head out of his own arse before we could do anything.

I'd rather not repeat this bit. It stung enough to tell it the first time. But John says the only way out of this for us is to tell you everything, to lay all our cards on the table. It's the only way you'll understand why we made the choices we did. How it ended up like this.

John believes in the system too much. Me? I don't trust you in the slightest. But I figure I've put him through enough that I at least owe him this.

Mark got up, started walking towards the lift. "I'm

leaving." He stopped, and looked back at me. "I should get out of this before I ruin anything else."

"Don't be an idiot. Everybody fucks up, Mark. Everybody. A lot of people fuck up a lot worse than this."

He stared at me for a long second. "Not you. You don't."

I nodded and then gave a deep sigh, because there was only going to be one way to get him over this.

"Yes—especially me."

DC Mark Cochrane: There's this look that Julia sometimes gets—like there's a ghost, or something that's haunting her, and she's trying really hard to forget about it, but now and again it pops up in front of her with full force and she can't look away. Her whole face sort of sets in stone like cement, except for her eyes. Her eyes look like they're melting. It's fucking terrifying.

Julia Torgrimsen: "When I was undercover, I did a lot of things that I regret." My voice was such a low whisper he had to come close and sit next to me. "That's part of being undercover—you have to be in the middle of the criminal activity, witness it, sometimes even take part in it to avoid suspicion. Eventually, I got so deep, I couldn't tell what was undercover and what wasn't."

I don't think I was even looking at Mark anymore. I couldn't. I stared out of Horner's window at the city below, waking in the morning light.

"I knew I needed a ridiculous amount of evidence to put someone like Yegorov away, so I placed myself at the centre of it all. I was basically his personal human-trafficking secretary—the one with all the notes, all the details. Now and again, I'd manage to help a few. I'd try and get one or two out without arousing suspicion, but it was nothing compared to what I was facilitating. A drop in the fucking ocean.

"There was this girl. Anna. She . . . she was one of the last in a line of girls that I'd forced myself to ignore for the case. I told myself, if I can nail this guy, if I can bring this whole operation down, from the top to the bottom, I'll save so many other girls it won't matter. But Anna . . ." Julia shakes her head. "There was something about her. I don't know, I can't put my finger on it. She had so much life in her, so much fight, despite her horrific circumstances."

Mark didn't say a word. He was in a kind of trance, mesmerised, and I was hoping he was starting to forget about his own fuckup, at least a little.

"Once it seemed like the case was finally starting to wrap up, I made her a promise. I promised her I would get her out, and when this was all over I'd find a home for her, even if she had to live with me for a while. That would be fine. I could probably do with the company. I didn't see her that often—she was being trafficked around the inner circle of all these billionaire fucks—and I'd be there to check in on her once or twice a week. Like a housekeeper. Like a fucking nanny.

"Except, each time I went, she'd get a little more urgent. She said it needed to happen quickly, that I needed to get her out straightaway. This week. I told her I couldn't, it wasn't quite time yet. I asked her what the problem was, but she never told me. She grew more and more insistent. She needed to get out. She *needed* to.

"But I kept putting it off. Another week, I told myself. There was another shipment of people coming in that I could photograph and document for evidence. There was another witness I could win over. Just another week.

"Always another week," I whispered. For a moment, I had to stop. I couldn't say anything else.

I looked over at Lilja, fists tight, pacing up and down in a corner. She was far away from us now, and I felt suddenly like I was caught up in this past moment and there was no escaping it. My chest felt tight. My hands shook.

"What happened to her?" Mark asked, and the question prompted the words out of me again.

"Eventually," I said, "she comes to me and tells me the truth. She's pregnant. The birth control I had her on had failed for some reason or another. And it's Yegorov's. No one could know, of course. I'd been telling Yegorov that I'd been sterilising them. That's what he wanted, so he didn't have to deal with any messy surprises, but I could never bring myself to do that. I just . . . I snapped at her. I screamed at her. Accused her of being selfish for not telling me, of being stupid for fucking up and getting pregnant, of I don't know what. It wasn't about her—it was my own guilt and sickness pouring out of me like poison. At the end, I told her I'd arrange an abortion. She told me not to. She wanted to keep it, she said. That's not possible, I said.

You said you'd get me out, she replied. *Now is the time. You promised.*

"She ended up having the child early—way too early. It was the stress, I think. I managed to keep her away from Yegorov and his thugs for a few months towards the end, but I knew it couldn't last. In all the time I'd known her, I'd never seen her so scared. If Yegorov found out that there was a child—*his* child—shit would hit the fan really quickly. If the child wanted any kind of life at all, it needed to be elsewhere. I couldn't trust that she would be able to keep quiet about it. She was too young. Too vulnerable. So after they took the baby away to be incubated, I told Anna that it had died."

"You—what?" Mark asked.

I grimaced. "Don't judge me, Mark. That's not the point here."

"No, I'm not. I just . . . that doesn't seem like you. That doesn't—"

"What the fuck do you know about who I am?" I snapped, my voice breaking. "You met me last night, Mark. You don't know the first thing about me. Now shut the fuck up and listen to the story."

Mark shrank away, the same way Anna had all those years ago. "Yes, ma'am."

"It felt like the only solution. The only way to keep Anna from doing something stupid, to give that baby a chance at a real life, away from all that. She would have to put it behind her. I arranged for the baby to go to an orphanage, temporarily, at least until the case was over. And you want to know the worst thing? I thought I'd done the right thing. I thought I'd made the right choice. But the truth is I was scared of Yegorov, and what he would do. Of how far his reach was, how furious his revenge would be.

"After I made the call to arrest Yegorov, the first thing I did was find Anna. I wanted to be the one to apologise, to tell her her baby did make it. That it was going to be okay. But it was too late. I should have seen it."

I blinked, surprised to find tears in my eyes, surprised I was still capable of that.

"Should have seen what?" Mark asked.

"I've seen bodies before. Too many. But . . . the blood running out of the bathtub. The empty look on her face."

I turned and grabbed Mark, pulling him towards me. "The point is *I did that*. I fucked up. I made the wrong call. It was my fault. Yeah?"

He blinked, his mouth opening and closing like a goddamn fish. "Er . . . maybe?"

"So what was I supposed to do next? Go hide in a hole, or do something about it?"

"What can you do? How do you fix something like that?"

"You don't. But you can sure as hell make sure that nobody else gets hurt. That's what you can do."

The look on his face—the resignation crusting over into newfound determination—it told me everything I needed to know. Jesus, the naive are so easy to manipulate. Then he reached inside his jacket. I said, "If you dare put a word of that story in your fucking notebook, I will rip your arms off."

With a sheepish look, he pulled his hand back out.

"Lilja," I said. She turned around, her face still fuming like someone had set it on fire. "How do we stop this?"

Mark nodded, wiping away some of the residual tears from his eyes. "Yeah, what can I do?"

"*You?*" she repeated, walking towards him. "There was no *you* in the original plan at all," she bit back. "It only needed two people. But now there's a fucking simulacrum out there that you didn't kill while it was still new and weak, and it will be hunting us the moment we travel through. We can't do this. It can't be done—it gets the jump on either of us alone and we're dead. Worse than dead."

I stood up, a plan falling into place. I walked into Horner's room and started looking around in the drawers. "Then we do it in teams of two. Each person watches the other person's back. If we see it, we kill it or we use the button to get out."

"We don't have two teams of two," Mark said.

Lilja shook her head. "And there isn't time to get more people. We have access to this machine *now*, but the moment the police show up, or anyone else does, the opportunity is gone. This machine will get shut down as tight as the other two. This won't work, Julia," she called after me. "Not with the three of us."

I opened the second drawer of the bedside table and found what I was searching for. Horner was still half-conscious, barely able to look up at me. I picked up the small black toiletry bag and stepped back into the living room.

"So we make it four." Both Lilja and Mark followed my line of sight, their eyes landing directly on John.

"Grossman?" Mark sputtered. "He's been shot. He's barely conscious."

"For now," I replied, opening the bag and pulling out a long needle. "In a moment, he'll have all the energy he needs."

Lilja blinked. "What are you going to give him—adrenaline?"

I grinned, reaching back into the bag and pulling out a bulging little plastic bag filled with white powder.

Mark stared at me. "Is that *coke*?"

I shrugged. "We're in a billionaire's penthouse, Mark. I'm using what I have on hand."

8

Julia Torgrimsen: I'd done this sort of thing before. I didn't like doing it—it brought back painful memories of administering drugs to trafficked boys and girls, keeping them addicted, keeping them controlled—but the situation wasn't new to me. Muscle memory took over.

I tied the tourniquet around his upper arm, letting a clear vein pop out.

I dabbed a little bit of the coke on my lips—it tasted clean, and as close to pure as anyone was going to find in London. I wouldn't need much to wake him up, to kill the pain. I didn't want to give John an overdose.

The white powder swirled as I crushed it into a small spoonful of water. John let out a quiet groan, his eyes still closed as I prepped the syringe.

"Sorry," I muttered, then stuck the needle in his arm.

DCI John Grossman: When I woke up, I *woke* up. It wasn't a slow, drowsy coming to reality. It was as if there was some kind of glass partition between unconsciousness and consciousness, and someone had grabbed the back of my head and smashed me through it face-first.

I was on my feet in seconds, my heart beating fast.

"Where am I?" I demanded. "What's going on?"

Julia was in front of me, and behind her was that blundering DC and that crazy killer girl who shot me.

Wait a goddamn second, I thought. *I've been shot.*

I looked down at my stomach, at the red-stained bandages wrapped around my waist, and I was surprised to find I wasn't feeling much pain. I wasn't feeling much at all, except this current of electricity that ran from my buzzing head right down to the tips of my fingers.

I stretched my fingers out, looking at them, examining them.

Have you ever thought about how long your fingers are?

"John," Julia muttered, and my eyes jerked up.

Oh, yeah.

There was a whole spectrum of crazy going on in that room that I had momentarily forgotten about.

I pointed at the girl. "Why is she not cuffed? Why is she just standing there?"

I took a step towards her, but Julia stood in my way. "A lot has happened here that you don't understand yet."

"She *shot* me, Julia!"

"I'm aware, John," she said, that infuriating know-it-all voice of hers. "I was there. There's no need to shout."

I blinked at her, trying to resolve this bizarre situation. It wasn't making any sense. "And *why* were you there? You're meant to be back at the station." I pointed at Mark. "He's meant to be watching you. Oh, you are so fired. You are more than fired. You are . . ." I grasped for the right word, but I couldn't get to it. Something wasn't quite right, and I wasn't sure if it was the blood

I'd lost, or the fact I'd been shot, but things were moving too quickly in my head. By the time I'd grasped onto one thought, it had catapulted me into another.

And the weirdest thing? I felt *great*. I felt like I'd won an Olympic medal. I felt like a superhero.

"Julia," I said, trying to keep my voice a little quieter. I was surprised to find myself sounding a little desperate. "What the hell is going on?"

Julia Torgrimsen: As I tried to explain everything to John, he paced back and forth like a caged tiger. He couldn't keep still. His fingers were twitching, his hands going to his face, his jaw gurning away like he was chewing on a three-day-old piece of meat.

He didn't speak much. He nodded occasionally, saying things like *yeah* and *okay, okay*.

I didn't know if it was the drugs, or whatever information he'd stumbled upon before he made it up to Horner's penthouse, but he was taking it all surprisingly well. When I told him about the time machine, he muttered, *"Sure, makes sense."*

Mark stood there, trying to be assertive and confident, but mostly just looking awkward. He sat down on the sofa and then got up again, crossing and uncrossing his arms. Lilja stood back and didn't say a word. She let me talk, but as I did I could see this strange look of pride growing on her face, like she knew she'd picked the right person for the job. It rankled me. I sympathised with her plight, but I didn't like being used like that, being manipulated. I'd had enough of that in my life.

When I'd got to the end, and how I woke him up,

there was a pause—a little silence of incredulity that emanated from John. He'd stopped pacing. He stared off into space, looking as though he was about to tell me I was insane, then he turned to me.

"I'm on *coke*?!"

"Ah," I said. "Yes. I needed to wake you up."

He burst out laughing. He bent over, holding his stomach, as the laughter roared out of him. The three of us stared at him, dumbstruck, as whatever private hilarity was going on in his head took its course. He struggled to breathe in between the sheer force of it.

Then he winced. His body curled inwards, and as he pulled his hands away from his stomach, they were red with blood.

The drugs helped kill the pain, sure, but it hadn't healed the wound.

Oh, well, I thought. He was the one that showed up at *my* flat.

Lilja took a step forward. "Do you understand what's happening here? Do you know what needs to be done?"

He waved a bloody, dismissive hand at her. "Oh sure, sure," he said, speaking very fast. "The four of us are going to travel to the past to steal and sabotage two time machines from a cabal of super-billionaires to prevent unseen galactic beings from causing the extinction of humanity, while trying to avoid being killed or tortured by a murderous alien doppelgänger version of Mark that wants to bring about the apocalypse. I got that right?"

She blinked. "Then what's so funny?"

"I knocked on Julia's door *yesterday*, and here we are. Jesus Christ." He shook his head, and a rueful smile appeared on his face. "Julia fucking Torgrimsen. It really never goes to plan with you, does it?"

Mark raised his head. "Actually, I knocked on her door. You were too scared to."

"*You,*" John said, pointing a direct finger at Mark, "can shut the fuck up."

DC Mark Cochrane: Am I thrilled Grossman's woken up? No, not entirely. I get that he's needed for this mission, or heist, or whatever you want to call it, to happen, but the guy treats me like shit. He has done ever since this started.

Sure—Julia hasn't exactly been cutting me much slack, either, but at least she's tried to help. Where the fuck was John when I was out of my depth and looking for guidance? I was doing the best I could.

So no, I wasn't exactly jumping for joy.

It's funny to think how much I looked up to him, a day or two before. It's funny how quickly your perception of things can change.

Is it funny? I don't know.

Maybe it's just sad.

DCI John Grossman: If I'm honest, my memory of that whole moment isn't as good as it should be. But I knew I'd had enough of standing around and talking. Maybe some part of me was aware that this bullet wound was actually going to need some serious attention at some point, maybe it was the coke making me impatient, but I wanted to be moving. I wanted to be *doing* something.

"Okay, let's get this show on the road then. Who goes with who? Do I get the idiot?"

Mark winced at that.

"No," Lilja replied. "He comes with me. Last thing I need is the two of you babysitting each other. Julia's the only other person I trust here to lead the other team." She turned to Julia. "I'll need my rifle back, but there's another gun in my bag for you."

"Fine," I said, happy not to have Mark to deal with. "When are we headed to?"

Lilja reached into her jeans pocket and pulled out a piece of paper. Unfolding it, she laid it out on the table in front of us. It was a map of London.

Julia Torgrimsen: "Five years ago," Lilja said, leaning over the map, "the other two machines were moved. They're kept in secret locations, inaccessible except by people like Donaldson. Security is far too high to be infiltrated. And they're never all three in transit at once. But at this one singular moment, *two* of them are—the other two that aren't this one.

"Here"—she pointed at two lines on the map—"are the routes they took. Both machines are in unmarked lorries. There's one armed security guard with the driver, but no one in the storage of the lorry itself."

"No one?" John repeated. "Seriously?"

"Security through obscurity," she replied. "The entire existence of these machines is a closely guarded secret. Only a handful of people know about them. Too much security and they look suspicious. The protection comes from secrecy, not from force. Now—the most obvious points to intercept are *here* and *here*. I've noted the times the lorries arrive. You can use the roadworks and the traffic lights to your advantage. You need to find a way to get to the machines inside."

"And destroy them," I said.

"No." She shook her head. "You can't do that. Those machines are still working now, in our current time. If you destroy them in the past, it'll change the timeline, set off a butterfly effect that will likely involve none of us even meeting here. We won't be able to destroy the third machine, the one here. The plan will be ruined."

I frowned. "So what do we do?"

Lilja opened her duffel bag and pulled out two small devices—about the size of a USB stick—and put them on the table. "This was the last thing my father developed before he died. A fail-safe that can be planted in the internal workings of the machine. If you hide them where I show you, they'll go undetected. They're tiny explosive devices I've set to blow up in five years' time, or, if placed in the past, about three hours from now. When that happens, the machines will be ruined irreparably and, without my father, they'll never be able to fix them. I'll put one in this machine, here, too, and they'll all go off at the same time. It's the only way to be sure."

"What about the other Mark?" I asked, glancing over at Mark scribbling the plan frantically down in his little notebook. He looked up sheepishly.

Lilja sighed. "If we're quick, and if we're very lucky, it might not be able to find us, but keep your eye out. It might look like Mark, but it'll be faster than you, stronger than you, and it won't die as easily as you. My bet is it'll try anything to get back here, including murdering you," she pointed at Mark, "and pretending to take your place. We need a code word. Something that simulacrum will never know."

Mark frowned. "Surely you'd know? I mean . . . I'm *me*."

Lilja gave him a hard look. "We've studied these things. When this thing copied you, it copied *all your memories*. It knows everything that makes you what you are. The only thing it won't know for certain is the specifics of what happened after the copy, but even then, it'll be damn good at improvising. We'll have to keep a close eye on every damn thing you say. When we ask you the code word, you need to say '*embarrassed elephants*.'"

"Embarrassed elephants?" he repeated. "Man, I'd never think of something like that."

She nodded. "Exactly."

As he looked back down at his notebook, I said, "Don't *write it down*, you idiot."

"Oh, yeah." He grimaced, tucking the notebook back into his pocket. "Sorry."

"Fine, fine, *fine*," John muttered, fingering the gun at his waist. "We get it. Scary and dangerous. Can we *go* already?"

I sighed, taking a deep breath.

This was going to be trickier than it looked.

DC Mark Cochrane: As we make our way back to the room with the machine, this sickening feeling grows inside of me. I know we're not going back to that horrific future, but I can't help it. With each step, I can feel my breathing getting heavier, I can feel my pulse quickening.

But I'd made my choice.

I was going to fix my mistake, whatever it took.

Julia went in first, and I followed her, with Grossman tailing right behind.

DCI John Grossman: I barged into that room first, propelled by some furious internal energy, and just stared at that big metal machine. A small part of my brain was telling me that I should be shocked at all this, even disbelieving, but it was overwhelmed by physical sensations. There was a buzz—a warmth that started in my chest and ran down my limbs to my feet, to the edge of my fingers. Despite the dull pain in my stomach, I had never felt so alive. That's all I could think about. What do I do with this kind of life? With this kind of energy? I couldn't wait to *do* something.

I was *really* high.

So when we enter a room with a giant metal contraption, and it starts whirring and opening to this bright pool of transcendent light, all I can think is *Here. We. Go.*

Julia Torgrimsen: At first, when we used the machine again, I didn't think anything had changed. The light came and went and we were in the same place, the same room.

But the machine was gone. The room was empty—the temperature different, the door behind us closed and we'd left it open. We hadn't moved location, but we had moved time.

Four and a half years.

Before I killed Yegorov. Before I'd caused Anna's death. Before everything.

"Take these buttons," Lilja said, passing us each one of those small contraptions we took into the future. "When you've planted the bomb, push the button to get back, but don't touch the machine *here* until we're all back or the other team will get stuck in the past. I've got suppressors for your weapons, too."

Mark frowned. "Why?"

Lilja hefted her rifle over her shoulder. She pulled out two keys from her duffel bag and handed one to me. "And you'll need this for the back of the lorry. And don't worry about this place—Horner isn't in right now. He's overseeing the transportation. We need to get to the access points. There are two cars in the parking garage on the ground floor. Can you hotwire a car?"

She was asking me, but before I had a chance to respond, John said, "I can."

I raised my eyebrows.

"What?" he asked. "You don't have a monopoly on being a badass, Julia. Just on being a massive *pain*."

I didn't reply. I just stared at him. He really wanted to laugh at his own joke. There was a smile already pushing its way to the corners of his lips.

DC Mark Cochrane: We're headed off in different cars, to two different intercept locations. Lilja isn't speaking to me. She isn't looking at me. Frankly, I'm okay with that. As far as I'm concerned she's still a crazed serial killer. I mean—yeah, sure, there's this end-of-the-world apocalypse thing taking place—but that doesn't mean I have to like her, and it definitely doesn't mean I have to trust her.

"How are we going to take the truck?" I ask.

She scowls, as if annoyed that she has to talk to me. "There's a set of roadwork lights at our intercept location. If we get there early, we can break them—keep them stuck on red. The truck will get stuck in the traffic. We can hide out in the shop next door until it gets there."

"What shop?"

She shrugs. "Some office furniture showroom, but it's a Sunday. Nobody will be inside. When the lorry is stopped, you watch the driver's seat to make sure nobody gets out. I'll break into the back and plant the bomb. It'll be over in minutes, provided you don't fuck up again."

I bristled. I wanted to tell her to shut up, that her attitude wasn't going to help us, but there was a big part of me that recognised she was right. It was down to me to not fuck up again. I needed to be better. Admitting that to yourself is difficult, though.

I fell back into my seat, crossing my arms and staring out the window as London of four years ago zoomed past.

DCI John Grossman: I was trying to tell Julia that we needed a plan. We couldn't zoom in guns blazing and hope for the best. I know what she's like.

Julia Torgrimsen: Every time I tried to lay out a fucking plan, John interrupted me.

"You realise there's a tunnel here?" he demanded,

his finger stabbing at the map. I hadn't let him drive, despite him being insistent that he could manage it.

"I *know* there's a tunnel, John. I was literally just telling you there's a tunnel there. If we can find some way of blocking the opposite end and trapping the lorry in the tunnel, then we've got both the cover of darkness and an enclosed space to infiltrate."

He was staring at the map. "A tunnel," he muttered. "Hold on. I'm getting an idea."

I sighed, my hand gripping the wheel.

"Wait, wait, wait. I've got it! What if we block off the end of the tunnel?"

I couldn't help it. I smacked him.

DCI John Grossman: Then she slapped me! Out of nowhere! I was trying to sort it out so we don't both die, and she starts assaulting me.

I rubbed my face, the skin sore where her hand had made contact. "You know," I said, "*this* is why nobody ever wanted to work with you."

DC Mark Cochrane: The shop is one of those showrooms for outfitting offices. Different corners have desks, all laid out with a mixture of office equipment and fancy ornaments and plants. There's a stone Buddha on one of the desks, making it look like the reception at a hotel resort in Thailand or something. It's all a little ridiculous.

I'm crouched down behind a filing cabinet with a direct view of the street ahead.

Every time I hear a sound—a creak of furniture, or

the burn of a car engine—I freak out. I keep expecting that *thing* to jump out at me. My hands are tight against the cabinet, holding on as if I might fall over if I let go.

There isn't much traffic, which is good because we don't need any onlookers seeing us break in and deciding to do something about it. The traffic lights are those temporary ones put up by road workers, but they're the automatic kind that are just left out. No one is actually manning them.

Lilja is fiddling with the electrics on one of them, fixing the wiring. Her rifle is by my feet so as not to attract too much suspicion, but the longer she takes the more nervous I get. She keeps checking her watch, and I check mine.

In a moment, she'll set the lights to be stuck on red. Three cars will arrive and line up in the queue, and then, in exactly four minutes and forty seconds, the lorry will arrive, fourth in the queue, with its back almost exactly lined up with the shop we're hiding inside.

She knows this, she says. She's studied the CCTV footage a hundred times. She's made the calculations.

The lights flick red. She turns to me and gives me a small thumbs-up, walking back towards the shop to hide with me.

It'll be okay.

She's planned this all out perfectly, I think, and allow myself a long, deep, calming breath.

A hand lands on my shoulder and I jerk around.

It's me, dressed in the exact same clothes I am.

It's *fucking me*.

"You should have listened to me, Mark," he says, and his fist collides with my face.

Julia Torgrimsen: The lorry should have been approaching any minute. The streets were quiet, thankfully, because we'd left our car sitting horizontally in the middle of the road at the end of the tunnel, blocking the exit. That—along with a few bins and a bench we found—should stop any vehicles simply driving through. That lorry wouldn't be going anywhere.

John was ahead of me, which I wasn't happy about, but he insisted that he lead the way. At least this way I could keep an eye on him. He was holding the keys that Lilja gave us and moving like he's a cartoon ninja or a spy or something. Idiot. We were crouched into the shadows on the side of the tunnel—out of the glare of the lights—trying to get to a good spot to wait.

I assumed we could leave the car, hoping that if someone moved it, the traffic would eventually continue on. There shouldn't be much impact on the future, that butterfly effect that Lilja mentioned.

I didn't really have much of a choice.

We stopped as the first car rolled up to our blockade. Just a normal woman. A civilian. She got out and looked at it, confused, then pulled her phone out to call someone. Another car pulled in behind.

After three cars had stopped, I saw the lorry coming down the tunnel.

"There it is," Grossman almost fucking shouted in my ear.

"*Shut up,*" I whispered, pulling him back into the darkness. I lifted my gun, pulling it close to me.

The lorry slowed down and stopped. I squinted, making out two figures sitting in the front, but it was too dark to see if they were men or women. Already, the others were arguing and shouting at one another by our blockade. One man was saying he was going to break into the car and move it himself.

I tensed, getting ready to move round to the back.

The door on the passenger side opened, and my heart stopped as Dmitri Yegorov himself stepped out and onto the pavement.

DC Mark Cochrane: My head hits the ground with a thump, and I can feel the blood pouring out of my nose. Again. *My fucking nose.* I mean, seriously. My face is never going to look the same ever again.

I fumble for my gun, but it's not there.

I look up. He's holding it in his hand.

How is he that quick? How is anyone that quick?

Just as he lifts the weapon, a stone Buddha flies across the room and smashes directly into his head with an almighty crack.

He collapses to the floor and Lilja appears right next to me.

"Get up," she mutters. "Where's my gun?"

I try to say, *He's got it,* but with my nose it comes out like *heshmmglurgl.*

Lilja lifts up her rifle and turns to where his body fell. But he's not there anymore. He's already gone.

"Shit," she mutters. "Three minutes."

"What?"

"The lorry gets here in three fucking minutes."

"Oh."

She shakes her head, exasperated, and starts walking through the furniture shop, rifle up, checking doors and corners.

I follow, but without a weapon I feel utterly useless. I bring my fists up in front of me, but I feel so completely stupid that I have to put them down again. Jesus Christ.

As I turn around, I see him—like looking in an impossible mirror—step out from behind a cupboard with my gun held high.

"FUCK!" is all I manage, and he fires. I throw myself at the floor and the shot goes wide. Lilja swings around and takes aim, firing twice.

The first bullet hits his shoulder and he grunts, jerking back. The second hits his hand, sending the gun clattering to the floor. Other than that, the bullets seem to barely hurt him.

Lilja darts at him, but he's too quick.

As she gets close, he leaps up onto one of the desks and rips down a ceiling fan—it goes tumbling straight towards her head.

She rolls out of the way, but he's already back on top of her—he moves *so fast*—the cord from the fan tight in his hands as he wraps it around her neck.

"Fuck," I say, again, pointlessly. She grapples with him, but he's too strong. She chokes and splutters, her arms flailing. And all I can think is that he's killing her. *I'm* killing her. That's what my face looks like killing someone. It's terrifying.

DCI John Grossman: *Oh, shit.*

That's literally all I thought in that moment.

Yegorov was *there*. The man himself, dressed in his snappy tailored suit. The mastermind, right in the middle of all of this.

She hadn't killed him yet. This was five years in the past.

I turned to look at Julia, because I suddenly had absolutely no idea what she was going to do.

Julia Torgrimsen: Four and a half years. Before the indictment and the trial, before I strangled him, before Anna.

Before Anna.

Before he got her pregnant, before I tried to cover it up, before she killed herself.

She was still alive, somewhere in this world. She still had hope. She still thought I was going to get her out.

And then it hit me:

I still could.

DCI John Grossman: Yegorov walked towards our blockade, slowly, cautiously, trying to work out the cause of the disturbance. And just as I was trying to think of something meaningful to say, like *It's okay, Julia,* or *This must be hard for you,* she took two steps forward and raised her pistol in the air, aiming directly for him.

DC Mark Cochrane: As I'm just fucking standing there, watching her getting choked out, this giant wave of anger washes over me. Anger at my own incompetence, my own fucking uselessness, at being confronted by the fact that whatever image of myself I have, at every stage of this journey I've been nothing but a hindrance.

I'm a loser.

The realisation bubbles inside of me and turns into an unspeakable fury at everything and everyone. Screaming, I run at the two of them.

The other Mark sees me running and tugs Lilja around like a human shield between us. I don't give a shit. Grabbing a small wooden desk, I hurl it at the two of them. Pencils go flying. Paper litters the air.

They're both knocked to the floor, but Lilja's free of the cord. She rolls over, coughing, hands at her throat. Mark—the *other* Mark—is already on his feet.

But I've got a stapler in my hand, and I slam it into his face.

His head jerks back, blood spurting out of his nose, and I laugh.

"Fucking hurts, doesn't it?" I scream, triumphant, just for a moment, then his fist punches straight into my throat.

I gasp, gurgling, but another blow is already coming. Fist upon fist—my stomach, my chest, my face.

I stumble back, falling onto my back, but he follows. I close my eyes, my hands go up to protect myself, but it's no use. He's a bulldozer. A force of nature.

Gunshots explode across the room. I open my bloody eyes to see that *thing*'s body bucking and shaking as bullets burst through him. Lilja's on her knees, holding her rifle, firing until her magazine goes empty.

He doesn't go down. He doesn't *go down*.

But he is seriously injured. He's shaking. He can barely stand.

Holding the blood that's pouring out of him, he stumbles backwards and runs, disappearing around a corner.

I get up, moving to follow, to chase after him, but Lilja grabs me.

"No," she says. "He doesn't matter. Look!" I follow her pointed finger to the lorry outside, now arrived, waiting at the lights. The driver has got out and he's on the phone to someone. "Go. That's all that matters. I'll make sure he doesn't come back."

I dash forward, grabbing the key and the USB bomb, and make for the lorry.

Crouching low, I move round the back. No one is looking at me. Everyone's focused on the lights. I thank whatever gods I can think of that Lilja put suppressors on the guns and that the windows look like they're double-glazed, or we'd have had the police on us already.

I can do this, I think to myself.

I can do this. I'm not a loser. I can fucking *do* this.

Quietly as I can, I unlock the lorry door, praying they don't notice it in the front. Pulling it slightly open, I dart inside.

It's pitch black. Fumbling for my phone, I turn on the torch, trying to remember exactly how to place this damned bomb that Lilja gave me.

Somehow, I do it.

Miraculously, I'm out of the door before anything goes wrong.

I close the lorry door and run back into the shop. Lilja is still waiting, rifle up, eyeing the periphery for any sign of my evil twin.

"You do it?"

"Yeah," I manage, breathlessly. "Yes."

DCI John Grossman: I threw my whole body at her, slamming into her before she could fire. We tumbled, rolling onto the ground.

"Get off me!" she seethed, kicking me away.

"You kill him, and the plan is ruined! Butterfly effect! Remember what Lilja said—when we go back, the other machine won't be there. None of this will happen!"

"I don't care!" Her face was red, her eyes wet. I'd never seen her so angry in my life.

"Extinction of the human race, Julia!" I said, getting to my feet, thinking about how I'm going to get her gun off her. "What's more important than that?"

"He is," she said, pointing at the distant figure of Yegorov.

I made a leap for her gun, but I was way too wide. The coke was throwing off my reaction times. She slapped me out of the way, kicking my leg out from under me. I slammed onto my back, the impact knocking the wind out of me.

"Don't do it," I panted, my voice breathless. "It's not worth it."

She didn't hear me. She was in some world of her own.

Lifting her gun again, she started walking towards Yegorov and I knew that this was it.

This was the end.

DC Mark Cochrane: "Shall we get out of here?" I ask. She smiles, and nods at me.

"You did good work there, Mark," Lilja says. "Well done."

And for some reason, despite the fact that I absolutely hate this crazy murderess of a girl, a warmth blossoms inside of me. I did it, and she couldn't have done it without me.

We both pull our return buttons out of our pockets, holding them in front of us.

"This is it?" I ask. "It's all over now?"

"As long as Julia did her job," she replies.

I smile, because of course she did. I'm certain of it. I've never been more certain of anything in my life.

"Let's go ho—" I start to say, but a figure leaps out from behind a filing cabinet, and slams straight into Lilja.

Him. The other Mark.

I stare, mouth open, as they grapple.

Too late, I realise what they're grappling for.

Mark gets his finger on her button and presses hard and both of them disappear, like they've flickered out of existence.

Oh, fuck, I think.

And then I do the only thing I can.

I press my own button and follow them.

9

DC Mark Cochrane: I reckon I snap back into the present just seconds after Lilja does. She's still grappling with that *thing*, the other Mark, and they're on the floor. Her rifle is still somewhere in the past. So is my gun. It's an almost equal matchup—his strength and power against her training. He seems to have her pinned down, but she wriggles free and gets in a hard kick at his face.

He staggers back.

"Destroy the machine!" Lilja shouts. "Now."

"Oh, yeah," I mutter, turning to look at it. "But how do I—"

"Open the panel at the back," she replies, but Mark is already closing in. "There's a—"

She has to dart back to dodge a punch that could crush chests.

I scramble for the back of the machine. There's a collection of tools on the ground—wrenches and screwdrivers and a bunch of other small pieces I don't recognise. There's also a crowbar. Maybe if I smash up the insides enough, it'll do the trick. Lilja lets out a yelp.

But a thought occurs to me. "If I destroy the machine," I shout, "can Julia and John make it back?"

"It doesn't matter!" she screams. "As long as they do their job, it doesn't matter."

But they'll be stuck in the past, I think.

I need to wait. I need to give her more time.

The other Mark has Lilja pinned up against the wall. Gritting my teeth, I pick up the crowbar and enter the fray.

Julia Torgrimsen: I don't think I was fully in control of my body anymore. Some reptilian part of my brain had stepped in and grabbed me, like a marionette, moving me inexorably forward.

I was going to kill him.

I was going to kill him before he could ruin Anna, before I hid her baby, before she killed herself, and then everything would be okay again.

"Julia!" John groaned from behind me. "Stop."

I didn't stop.

I didn't even consider stopping.

DCI John Grossman: Julia's probably not going to tell you this bit. I don't know if it was the coke, or the heat of the moment, but as I watched her about to shoot Yegorov and ruin the entire mission, one thought blazed utterly clear in my mind.

"For Christ's sake, Julia," I said. "Don't be so fucking *selfish*."

Her whole body froze. Turning around, her face seethed with fury. She stormed back towards me, leaning down to look me right in the eyes.

"*What?*"

"I . . ." I started, but she didn't give me the chance.

"What the fuck did you say to me? I'm doing this for

Anna. I'm doing this for all the girls that died because of him."

"No," I said. "You're not. If we don't complete this mission, the extinction still happens." I pushed myself up onto my knees, desperately trying to get through to her. "Listen to me, Julia. You can't kill him. You kill him and the whole timeline is different. Extinction still happens. If you stop Yegorov now, she *still* dies. We all do. This doesn't help anyone. This just absolves *you*."

Her mouth set into a hard, thin line. "I don't care."

"You're going to ruin everything. You're going to destroy the world."

"I already ruined everything!" she screamed. I winced, hoping that we wouldn't be heard over the rumble of engines in the tunnel. She didn't seem to care. "Where do you think I've been the past four years, John? What do you think I've been doing? I already fucked everything up because of the choices I made, because of the things I did." She spun to point at the figure of Yegorov off in the distance, now on the phone with someone and shaking his head. "Because of *him*. Earlier today, I told Mark that you can't fix something like that. That I couldn't save Anna. But now I *can*, John. I can save her."

"And doom the rest of humanity," I replied, but she barely heard me.

"I can save her," she repeated, turning to leave me behind. "Don't try to stop me."

DC Mark Cochrane: I swing the crowbar right at his head, and he twists. He *catches it*, like it's a pool noodle or something, and twists it away from me.

Great.

But it gives Lilja the opening she needs. Ducking low, she leaps at his waist and tackles him out of the room, tumbling through the door and into Horner's upstairs flat. I follow, panting, my whole body aching.

Horner is just *there*. Having somehow freed himself, he's standing by one of the office seats. He's making a pot of coffee, the jug under the machine whirring as it slowly fills up.

He's got a mug in one hand and a gun in the other.

He lifts it up when he sees us, but doesn't know where to shoot.

Lilja is on top of the other Mark, grappling with him on the floor, and Horner's watching them, looking from one to the other. She grabs a keyboard from the desk, smashing it into the simulacrum's head, over and over until it's a mess of wires.

"Fucking shoot him!" I shout at Horner.

Horner looks to me, then back at the simulacrum, and a sudden realisation spreads across his face. He takes two steps forward, pointing the gun at the two of them grappling on the floor, and fires.

The simulacrum pulls Lilja right in front of him just in time.

The bullet explodes through her chest, a splatter of red spurting out the other side. She falls on top of the other Mark, who pushes her to one side.

Horner shoots again, but the simulacrum isn't pinned down anymore. He's too quick. He dodges and rolls to his feet, charging at Horner.

I throw myself at him, but I'm too slow, missing him entirely and rolling across the floor.

Idiot, I think. But there's nothing I can do.

Before I have time to even think about moving again, the other Mark has closed the distance between him and Horner, slapping the gun out of his hand.

He takes Horner's head and slams it into the wall.

Again, and again, and again, each one ringing with a sickening crunch.

He must have been dead after the first couple, but the simulacrum keeps going, like a factory machine that doesn't know how to stop, until all that's left on top of Horner's neck is a shattered smudge of brain and bone fragments.

"Oh God," I mutter, using the table to clamber to my feet. The bile rises in my throat. The other Mark turns to look at me, his face a painting of cold calculation.

Julia Torgrimsen: I was about fifty metres away from him when I decided I was close enough not to miss. Still obscured by the darkness of the tunnel, I pointed my pistol back at Yegorov and put my finger on the trigger.

He turned, clearly annoyed at the holdup, and waved at the driver of the lorry to get out and help him.

It's no use, I thought. *I've got you now.*

But then the door opened.

The driver got out.

It was me.

And then it all came back to me—I'd been here before,

in this tunnel, with this roadblock. I'd forgotten it because it was so inconsequential, so long ago. Yegorov had told me he needed someone he trusted to drive a lorry. I'd never even asked what was in it.

I watched as he lifted a single finger and made a *come here* gesture, like he was giving orders to a child. And I watched as I *did it*. Without question, or comment. I walked straight over to him, like a fucking pet being told to heel.

I wanted to throw up. I wanted to shoot myself, for being such a spineless idiot, thinking that I was making my own choices when I was so completely under his control.

And then it hit me: I was still under his control.

Four years of wallowing in my own hatred and self-pity, and all it took was the sight of him to throw every other choice and decision out of the window. There I was, willing to sacrifice the rest of the human race, because of how much control he had over my mind and my body.

This doesn't help anyone, John had said. *This just absolves you.*

I thought I was doing this for Anna, for all the people that I hurt, but I wasn't. I was doing it because nothing had changed. He still owned me.

"Let it go," John whispered. He was standing right behind me, and his words sent a shiver down my spine. "That's not you anymore, Julia. You've done your penance. Let him go."

I took a deep breath, the salty taste of my tears dripping into my mouth, and I lowered the gun.

As I turned around, John put his arms up to envelop me in a hug.

"Oh, fuck off," I said. "We've still got a job to do."

He smiled, then gave me a hard nod. "You go. I'll keep an eye on them. I trust you."

And with that, I was on the move.

DC Mark Cochrane: He walks towards me, slowly, like he knows there's nothing I can do. Horner's gun is on the floor behind him, but there's no way I can get to it without getting through him.

I turn around, scrambling on the desk for some kind of weapon—a knife, a heavy ornament, *something*. But there's nothing.

He's right behind me when my eyes land on the coffee machine, jug now full with almost two litres of boiling black liquid.

I grab the handle and spin, throwing the entire thing right into his face.

He screams, hands thrown upwards as his skin sizzles, and I take the moment to shove him backwards.

He stumbles, tripping over Lilja's body, and falls on his back.

There's just enough time for me to pick up Horner's gun and place the muzzle directly on his forehead.

"Get out of my fucking body," I say, and I fire.

I've got to say, despite everything else that's happened today, there's nothing quite as weird as watching your own head explode.

DCI John Grossman: By the time Julia got back to me, I was feeling really rough. It had started around the time she tackled me to the floor, and it was getting worse and worse. I was shivering, goose bumps rippling their way up and down my arms. My head ached. My gut felt like it was about to heave.

Turns out that's what a comedown feels like.

Then the pain returned—in my stomach, where the bullet wound was. It was like a searing hot poker had been pressed into me and was just getting hotter and hotter with every moment. I was sitting on the floor, leant back against the tunnel wall, and my vision was starting to get a bit blurry.

"John," she whispered, making her way over to me. "Are you okay?"

"Not really."

"You need medical attention."

"What I need," I said, "is to get back to the present. Is it done?"

She nodded. Putting my arm around her shoulder, she lifted me up and pulled out the return button from her pocket.

Julia Torgrimsen: I don't know what we expected to see when we got back, but it definitely wasn't what we saw. The bookcase door through to the office room was open, and there was Mark, so completely covered in blood he might as well have been bathing in it, and surrounded by dead bodies. Lilja, Horner, and a bloody copy of himself.

"Oh, Christ," John groaned, and threw up, the contents splattering onto the ground, and my feet. Lovely.

"What the fuck happened here?" I asked, lifting my gun and pointing it at him.

Mark turned around. "Julia? Jesus—I . . . what are you doing?"

"Lower your weapon," I said. My eyes narrowed, looking at him closely, looking at the scene around him. The blood. The bodies. "What's the code word?"

"What?"

"The code word, Mark—what is it?"

DC Mark Cochrane: Would you actually believe—and I'm being completely honest here—that I forgot? I mean, there I am, I'd watched two people die and I'd been forced to kill a weird alien clone of myself. I'm battered, bruised, and swimming in blood, who knows how much of it is my own. There's a gun in my face and I just fucking *blanked*.

"Use the code word," Julia repeats.

"I don't—"

"USE THE CODE WORD!" she screams, and it doesn't help one bit, because I know—I mean, I just absolutely *know*—that she's going to kill me.

Julia takes two deliberate steps towards me and lifts the gun slightly, aiming it right at my head. "Get on your knees."

My hands are shaking. My whole body is shaking. How much blood have I lost? *Okay*, I think to myself. *Just do as you're told. Maybe it'll come back to you.*

I bend my knees slowly, starting to kneel, but my ankle locks and buckles underneath me. My foot catches in a pool of blood and slips away. My whole body jerks forward, face hurtling towards the floor.

Then pain.

So much pain.

Julia Torgrimsen: He face-planted into the bloody ground so hard, you'd have heard the wet slap in the next room. For fuck's sake. If anything was going to confirm it was the real Mark, it would be that. It was like something out of a Looney Tunes cartoon.

He rolled onto his back, clutching his face, moaning. I inched forward, still wavering between keeping my gun on him and coming to his aid, when the machine started beeping.

"What the hell is that?" John asked. He was still on the floor next to the beeping contraption, looking greyer and greyer with every second.

From the floor, a burble came out of Lilja's throat. It was mostly blood, an incomprehensible sound gargling through as her eyes flickered briefly back to life.

"I think," I said, "that's the bomb she planted."

John looked at the machine—a couple of feet away from him—and blanched. "Oh, shit."

He scrambled forward, crawling and slipping in the bloody floor to get clear. I darted to him, grabbing his arm and pulling him towards me. He was so weak, like a dead weight.

Mark was just lying there, clutching his face, staring at the machine. Useless.

So yeah, again—definitely Mark.

I gave an almighty heave, falling backwards as John toppled over on top of me with a grunt and the machine burst into flame.

It started small—a tiny flicker of fire before the smoke started billowing heavily out.

Mark scrambled over to Lilja's almost-dead body, bringing her face up to his. "Is that it? Is it over? What about the others? The other machines?"

She burbled again, weakly, and for a flicker of a second I thought I saw fear in her eyes, or worry, before her head lolled back and her face glazed over.

I pushed John off me and he rolled onto his back with a moan.

Then a phone started ringing. Not me. Not John or Mark.

I tracked the sound over to Horner's body—trying not to throw up at his absence of a head—and plucked his phone out of his jacket pocket. The screen was cracked and I couldn't see the number.

I picked up the call and put it to my ear, not saying a word.

"Norman? Norman—are you there? It's the project. The machines. They . . . I don't know what happened. Both of them! There was fire and then smoke and then . . . They're ruined, Norman. Ruined!"

I smiled.

"That's it," I said, dropping the phone to the floor. "It's over."

Mark slumped back in relief, though I'm not quite sure I could actually discern his facial expression after the beating he'd given himself. With his swollen, bruised face and mangled nose, he almost looked upset.

John looked up. "Can someone call me a goddamn ambulance now?"

DCI John Grossman: Julia called in to the station on my phone, which she still had, by the way, and got ambulances and a police escort on the roads immediately.

"What do we tell them?" Mark asked.

"The truth," I said. I was struggling to breathe a little, but I could still get my words out and this was important. "We tell the full story. Everything from beginning to end."

"They won't believe us," Julia muttered.

I shook my head. "Doesn't matter. If we're all consistent, if we're all honest, we'll be fine. Given the circumstances, I think we'll be okay. But we can't leave anything out."

Julia scoffed, shaking her head at me like I was an idiot. "You've got too much faith in the system."

"I know," I said. "That's what separates us, Julia. Even after everything that's happened, that's what's always separated us. You might be the smartest detective I know, but that's what makes me a better officer. Faith."

Julia Torgrimsen: Faith, he says. Be fucking honest. Great. As if words ever changed anything. As if this was some kind of happy ending. Sure—we'd stopped an immediate apocalypse, but there was still an extinction event coming in four hundred years' time. We hadn't stopped that. We still had no idea what those clones even wanted.

But I agreed, more for his sake, and Mark's, than anything. I agreed to tell you guys everything that happened. I did it for Lilja's sake too—she died not knowing if the plan had worked. Her father's plan. She deserves some recognition.

But it doesn't mean I had to stand there right then and listen to him talking bullshit. Fuck that. Let the ambulance deal with him. I was going home.

DCI John Grossman: She just left. Well, not quite. She still managed to spit on Horner's dead body on the way out. Mark stayed with me until the authorities showed up. He was good, helpful even, considering the way his face looked. He explained everything he could to them, got the bodies zipped up and taken away, handled them like a pro.

I couldn't help but wonder if the Mark of yesterday could have done that. Sometimes experiences like this can change you for the better, even with all the trauma that comes with it.

Before they took me away, I called Mark over. He was still holding on to that bloody notebook of his like it was some kind of Bible.

"Don't blame Julia for how she acts," I said. "She's always been like this a little bit, but, well . . . you know about Anna."

He frowned, looking at me a little confused. "Who?"

I blinked. I could have sworn she said she told him. But maybe I'm remembering wrong.

"Don't worry about it," I said. "Just the drugs talking."

After all, it had been a *very* long day.

ACKNOWLEDGMENTS

This one was a blast to write, guys. Honestly. But I couldn't have done it without some very important people. As ever, I'm constantly in adoration of my wonderful wife, Allys, much as I am of the screaming, dancing, singing, storytelling, *hilarious* messes that are my two children.

This book also wouldn't be this book without Lia Holland, Eleanor Imbody, and Talia Rothschild. Thanks also to David Goodman, who knows more about guns than he should, especially for someone who assures everyone he is *not* a "gun guy."

While I'm getting quite good at getting these words out of my brain via my fingers, it wouldn't make its way into your hands without the hard work of my agent, Alex Cochran, my editor, Lee Harris, and the whole team at Tor. Thanks to them for all their hard work.

And thanks to you, readers, for making the story worth telling.

ABOUT THE AUTHOR

Allys Elizabeth Photography

NICHOLAS BINGE's work has been featured in *The New York Times, The Sunday Times, The Wall Street Journal, Financial Times, Entertainment Weekly, The Washington Post,* and more.

His work has been translated into eleven languages, and multiple works are in development for film and television. *Ascension,* a *New York Times* Editor's Choice Pick, has been hailed as a must-read "5-star horror novel" by Stephen King and was a nominee for the 2023 Goodreads Choice Award for Best Science Fiction novel. His last novel, *Dissolution,* described as an "expertly crafted puzzle" by *New Scientist,* released to international critical acclaim.